Heat the Grease, We're Frying Up Some Poetry

Copyright © 2019 Gnashing Teeth Publishing. All rights reserved.

All writers retain copyright to their work. No duplication or reuse of any selection is allowed without the express written consent of the writer.

Original Front Cover Art by Jennifer Taylor

Original Back Cover Art by Brody Williams
www.brodywilliamsart.com

The font used is Bahnschrift for ease of reading for those with dyslexia.

Editor-in-Chief Karen Cline-Tardiff

Copy Editor Jennifer Taylor

Printed in the United States of America

ISBN 978-1-7340495-0-3

Fiction: General

Fiction: Anthology

Editor's Invitation to Feast

Food is a common thread through all civilizations. Whether it be eating or preparing meals, ceremonies surrounding food, the memories which food evokes, food is the one thing which ties us all together. The recipe from an old friend, now passed, helps a woman to open her heart. A man recalls, fondly, preparing dinner with the woman he loves. A grandfather teaches gratitude for abundance with food cooked over a campfire. A relationship is forged over an herb cutting. This anthology is meant to bring us all together at the same table, a poetic feast surpassing any race or ethnicity, uniting old and young. The poems and flash fiction presented here remind us we are all, at our best and at our worst, just human.

This delicious anthology surrounding food represents 91 authors from 10 countries on 4 continents, proving that food truly is the tie that binds. Whether it be something sweet or savory, we encourage you to dig in and enjoy!

Karen Cline-Tardiff
Editor-in-Chief, Gnashing Teeth Publishing

Karen and I first met in a creative writing class, in high school, hmffmf years ago. I was the new kid, and Karen and her group of friends embraced me and gave me a place to belong. It was, it turns out, one of the most fortuitous days of my life, as several undying and priceless friendships sprouted from that one class. In more recent years, Karen and I have bonded further over our shared love of food and cooking. So, when she asked me to come on board as editor at Gnashing Teeth Publishing and told me what our first project would be, it felt like jigsaw puzzle pieces snapping into place.

I immediately had a vision of what I wanted the anthology to be, or rather, what I didn't want it to be. I knew I didn't want it to contain too much "chicken soup for the soul" because...well...that niche is already filled. But, also, it was because food is part of our every day lives. This means that it is part of not only family and celebration, but also grief, sex, isolation, control, illness, and everything else that comprises the human experience. Indeed, sometimes, the most significant thing about food, in one's life, is the lack thereof. So, while I did want joy and nostalgia, I also wanted radical honesty and a little bit of darkness. To that end, our submitting authors did not disappoint.

The authors I have included here put their hearts on paper and graciously shared them with us. I have grown intimately familiar with each work in this anthology. The pieces which brought me to tears, made me catch my breath, or tickled me, the first time I read them, still do so today. I have been so honored to be entrusted with this task, and so humbled by the talent between these pages. Thank you, reader, for allowing us to share these delectable offerings with you. Bon Appétit!

Jennifer Taylor
Editor, Gnashing Teeth Publishing

Iris N. Schwartz, "Tainted" (originally published in the journal Idle Ink, September 24, 2018) and "Folie a Deux" (originally published in Pure Slush: GLUTTONY 7 Deadly Sins Volume 2, June 2018).

Caroliena Cabada "How to Grow Basil" was originally published in *Barren Magazine*.

Elaine Reardon, "Hye Holiday Gathering" was originally published in Baugatuk River Review, Summer/Fall 2019.

Joanne Jagoda, "Mr. Avocado Man" was originally published in Gemini Magazine, August 2015, and nominated for a Pushcart Prize.

Julia Wendell, "Letting the Cat Out" was originally published in *Take This Spoon* (Main Street Rag Press).

Heat the Grease,
We're Frying Up Some Poetry

Table of Contents

Title	Author	Page
How to Cook a Poem	Juleigh Howard-Hobson	1
Coriander Fingers	Raven Sky	2
Hail to the Cook	John Grey	4
Perspicacity	Juleigh Howard-Hobson	5
All Hallows' Eve Delights	Eduard Schmidt-Zorner	6
Hye Holiday Gathering	Elaine Reardon	9
My Grandmother's Kitchen Fifty Years Later	Deborah Purdy	11
Pancakes and Steak	Linda Crate	12
Textbook Dualism: The Lowcountry Boil	Johnny Masiulewicz	13
Family Dinner	Neil Davidson	14
Aria for Arborio	Mark Fleisher	18
Mussels	Kirsty A Niven	19
Breakfast/The Boil/Mom's Day	Jackie Anderson	20
Homecoming	Jennifer Rood	21
Stir	Cambria Hines	22
Better Than Breakfast	DS Maolalai	23
Pie	Catherine Edmunds	24
Edible Flowers	Bruce Meyer	25
Beetroots	Naida Mujkic	29
Winchell's	Michael Neal Morris	30
Pyrrhic Donut Victory	Leah Mueller	32
Long Hot Summer Sundays	Sarah Evans	35
Marble Hill	Brian J. Alvarado	36
Hummus	Jeff Burt	37
Mustard and Cress	Stephanie Pressman	38
Dreaming While Fasting	Merridawn Duckler	39
Haute Cuisine in Mythology	Mikal Trimm	40
Firsts and Lasts	John Biggs	41
Prepping Paella	Diane Kendig	43
Burnt Rice	Shelly Rodrigue	44
What I Don't Expect	Elizabeth Beck	45
Broken Spanish in the DR	Shelly Rodrigue	46

Tonic	Ann Cefola	47
Coleystown, October 1971	Jonathan B Aibel	48
Mr. Avocado Man	Joanne Jagoda	49
Viands	Vivian Wagner	51
Tomatoes	Joan McNerney	52
Counter Espionage	Jeff Burt	53
For the Love of Chili	Yrik-Max Valentonis	55
Nightshade	Bruce Meyer	58
Aubergine	Sharon Munson	60
Friday Afternoon at Mahane Yehuda Marketplace	Sharon Munson	61
Friday Before Shabbat	Michael Mahgerefteh	63
Two Independence Days	Nicole Taylor	64
Kitchen Witch	KB Baltz	67
From Apples to Apple Butter	Sandy Green	68
Cucumber Work	Johnny Masiulewicz	70
Cake	Christopher Mitchell	71
All the Way to That Way	DS Maolalai	75
Dysphagia	Jane Blanchard	77
Cast Iron	Natalie Illum	78
Capital Nourishment	Brian J. Alvarado	79
Pasta in the Nude	Barrett Warner	80
A Brief Blinding	Michael Neal Morris	82
Dreaming of William Carlos Williams at a Vietnamese Restaurant	Leah Mueller	83
At the Chinese Restaurant	Keli Osborne	84
Random Recipes: Curried Pterodactyl with Fried Bananas	Yrik-Max Valentonis	85
Nuts	Joe Williams	86
Jolting	Jack M. Freedman	87
Ode to Margarine	Ginger Lee Thomason	88
Affront to a Madeleine	Keli Osborn	89
How to Cook a Moon	Kersten Christianson	90
The Sanctity of Bread	Lauren Cutrone	91

Ode to a Kitchen in Connecticut	Suellen Wedmore	93
Butter Me Up	James Gering	96
Morning Prayer	Todd C Truffin	97
How to Eat an Omelette	Edward Vidaurre	100
5 senryu	Dr. Ronald K Craig	101
Ode to my Cast Iron Frying Pan	Suellen Wedmore	102
To Grandmother's Fallout Shelter We Go	Christine Collier	104
Mama's Silver	Larry Pike	107
Blessed Meals During Cursed Times	Bob McNeil	109
Things They Never Said I'd Miss	Shelly Rodrigue	110
Tamales Mean You've Arrived	Elizabeth Beck	111
Lunch Lady	Elvis Alves	112
During the Butchering	Stephanie Pressman	113
Black Meat Chef	Karla Linn Merrifield	115
How to Slow Boil Your Twin's Heart for a Hearty Munch	Hiya Mukherjee	116
Acquired Tastes	Bruce Meyer	119
Cold Carrot Curry	Joan Leotta	121
How to Grow Basil	Caroliena Cabada	123
The Rages of Garlic is Love	Cynthia Gallaher	126
Oregano Has Left the Restaurant	Cynthia Gallaher	128
Night Kitchen	Glen Armstrong	129
Savour	Sarah Jane Justice	130
Ham and Legs	Shane Moritz	131
Rhonda Threw a Reuben On	Les Epstein	133
The Legacy of Jose Padilla	Matt McGee	135
Salt and Vinegar	Fern G. Z. Carr	137
Crispy, Crunchy, Gone	Mark Fleisher	139
The Invitation	Justin Hunter	141
First the Slaughter	Justin Hunter	142
How to Fry a Daughter	Amy Barnes	143
The Mistress of Staggering	Cath Nichols	146
Recipe	Merridawn Duckler	147

Folie a Deux	Iris N Schwartz	148
Bones	Jaclyn Piudik	151
What We Put in our Mouth Matters	Raven Sky	153
Porridge	Agnieszka Filipek	157
Eating Oatmeal	Diane Kendig	158
Weekly	Temitope Ogunsina	159
Oyster	Joe Williams	160
A Memsahib Learns to Cook	Sahana Ahmed	161
Regarding Damir	John Grey	163
Tainted	Iris N Schwartz	165
One Half Egg Shell of Water	Joanne Jagoda	168
Making Mayonnaise	Terry Alan Kirts	173
Seasoning	Deborah Purdy	175
Snake Soup	Marlee Head	176
Mulberries	Tom Daley	179
Suppertime	Carl "Papa" Palmer	180
Cooking for the Cat	Janet McCann	183
A Student Supper	Adrian Slonaker	184
Reimagining Olives	Shelby Lynn Lanaro	186
Thanksgiving	Jonathan B Aibel	188
Letting the Cat Out	Julia Wendell	189
Twenty Ways Cooking is a Liability to my Love Life	Terry Alan Kirts	191
Breakfast Poem	Samuel Swauger	193
Cookbook	Stephanie Pressman	194
Skillet	Jackie Fox	199
Afghani Chicken	Debjani Mukherjee	200
All the Souvenirs	Agnieszka Filipek	202
Barbecued Poem	Louise Hofmeister	203
Cornbread Without Butter	André Wilson	205
Cornbread Without Butter Sheet Music	André Wilson	207

How To Cook a Poem
A recipe for *les sonnets sucre*

For truly poetic food, you must look
Beyond *à la mode*. Cookies are good, I've
Found. People like them, they're pleasant to cook.
Preheat your oven to three twenty-five.
Cream two cups of butter, softened, with one
Cup of brown sugar, packed. Add four cups of
All-purpose flour. Mix. Turn out upon
A nonstick board. Knead. Make sure that enough
Classic form holds while you carefully roll
The dough in fourteen lines. Slice each one ten
Times. Place on ungreased bake sheets. Check the whole
Batch for any faults, then place in oven.
Bake five minutes, until gold. You will get
Beaucoup des biscuits and one sweet sonnet.

Juleigh Howard-Hobson – Washington, US

Coriander Fingers

you're my favourite flavour
the cool, creamy relief of raita on my fiery, complex curry
the queer, sour saltiness of green olives on my piping hot pizza
the sweet chill of caramel ice cream on my steaming cinnamon
apple crisp

you, my love
you are the simple power of fresh herbs' flavour
you are the pretty presentation

you fill my mouth, my eyes, my belly
with warmth and desire
you make my toes wiggle with joy

you are hot chocolate stirred patiently on the stove
tea with whole spices steamily brewing
you are really real just squeezed orange juice
your authenticity and soulfulness inspire me
i want to serve the world as faithfully as you

see i once thought womanhood
entailed slapping on a uniform
and being run ragged catering to others
who checked out your ass
while yelling at you for not fulfilling their orders
i would not be that woman
and so i ran away and shrank away
to an angry but free sack of bones
till you came along
and insisted i nourish myself

gave me more, always more, than i thought i needed
and i began to fill out
to risk the vulnerability of breasts and hips
i found the mad urge of craving

and the tender desire of pleasing another's mouth
the ones you love

so now chopping is not a chore
but a moving meditation
an act that connects me to millions of
other women in other countries other kitchens other times
working to bring pleasure to those they treasure
women and food
an ancient connection
for cooking is cosmic
i stir the pot
the earth mother stirring a cauldron of possibilities
sustaining life
in such mundane daily acts of artistry

you stick me in no uniform
you demand nothing of me
except my own fulfillment
and in awe i discovered mine came in time with yours
you who came to me with the scent of cilantro on your fingertips
and a full-bellied laugh in your mouth

Raven Sky – Canada

Hail to the Cook

Recipes never die.
Sharp and clean
and to the point,
they behave so much more
clearly than memory.
My mother, the cook,
I break off pieces of her life
and eat them,
sizzling steaks and
strings of spaghetti
my fork battles
like trout with hook.
And always the lemon meringue pies
that sunned on window sills
like bathing beauties,
tempting my pacing eyes and tongue.
The old woman
shuffling through the rooms
in her house coat
in ever decreasing circles
left us a hundred dollars
and a government bond.
Ah but the recipes,
like photo-albums
of simmering stews,
boundless salads,
succulent pies,
delectable casseroles...
years later,
I thumb through them
with my tongue.

John Grey – Rhode Island, US

Perspicacity

Apples do not last once they are bitten
The edges ooze and soften slowly through.
Eaters wet the skin with juices, fitting
Cool flesh to warm behind them as they chew.

In defiance of ancient mysteries
Nuns don't mind picking fruit from apple trees.

The essence of each apple has two parts:
Outer, which is, of course, the first impressed
Upon the mouth, and inner, which imparts
Delights of its flesh to those whose tongues wrest
Them from the core. Sisters, with cloistered hearts,
May only guess which portion Eve liked best.

Juleigh Howard-Hobson – Washington, US

All Hallows' Eve Delights

The ploughed fields mark the end of the harvest season and the beginning of winter, the 'darker half' of the year. This is the liminal time, when the boundary between this world and the Otherworld thins.
The umbrella of the night sky spans overhead, where millions of stars have been shining for billions of years, on this reoccurring *Samhain*, the "first day of winter", the half point between equinox and solstice.
This transition from one day to the other. And this night in between, where a curtain slides to the side and we get an insight into the pagan grounds of our souls, into a subconscious, dulled and immunized by the harsh light of modern paraphernalia and glitz, weaned from the mysterious and inexplicable.
A temptation felt to camouflage oneself to ward off evil and to pretend one is not there.
The darkness falls within minutes and the mind needs tranquilization, a sedation. To retire into the kitchen, where, witchlike, soup and sauces are stirred, frying pans filled and the oven preheated.
The smell of the season, the scent of fried onions permeates the house. They sizzle, the outer skin crackles, disintegrates into the next layers, they caramelize with sugar and are accompanied by boletus mushrooms, milk caps and morels.
The shoulder of mutton is larded with half cloves of garlic and the steamed pears in butter are bedded between boiled green beans, marjoram, mustard, caraway, parsley and chervil with added pumpkin seeds. Turnips cleaned, juniper berries crushed, tripe cut down into finger length strips.
The oven serves as source of hope and revelation.
It is good to step outside the door during such a mysterious night.
There is the call of a screech owl, and something rustles in the bushes. Should sacrifices be offered to unknown spirits, food and drink, samples of the crops, a glass of wine poured over

the meadow or seeds sprinkled? Or *báirín breac*, potato cake, champ or colcannon kept ready? In an earthen bowl to please the unknown creatures?
The dog starts to growl. He knows more and hears more. He is related to spirits, wolves, fairies and elves. Or are there already the beings of the Otherworld who want to get in touch, make themselves noticed or make fun of us?
But it is only a late bird. It rises from the undergrowth with flapping wings and flies through the branches.
The bite into the apple that ripened on the tree behind the house, its bitter-sweet taste sharpens the senses.
Behind the roses walks a white figure and soon a cloud gives way to the moonlight, which the half-fat waning moon, pours like milk over the garden.
Are all the forgotten and rejected gods angry with us because we have cooked them together into one God, like a soup made of noble ingredients and spices and fine vegetables?
A shuffling of steps on the country road behind the wall awakens curiosity to check out who walks there. The road is empty.
Was it the neighbour who died last year? During this night the souls of the dead revisit their homes seeking hospitality. He liked his daily walk.
Only bushes, trees and a scarecrow form a changing background, a backdrop where shadows and branches move like excited actors, who have forgotten their script.
Conversations behind the blackberry hedges can be heard, laughter and crying... the otherworld gathers together, the aos sí, the supernatural...
The dog sniffs at something which is invisible and looks with assuring eyes and signals "No danger".
The horizon shows a small golden strip, bonfires are lit. Their smell of smoke with purifying powers levitates over the surrounding land.
Not to forget to set places at the dinner table and by the fire to welcome the souls of the dead which return home on one night of the year and must be appeased.

The steam from the pots may make them visible to the human eye.
A few apples and a handful of nuts, signs of immortality and divine wisdom, frame the dinner plates. Cinnamon is powdered over them in the hope to side-track the ghosts by the perfume.

roasting hazelnuts
reveal name of future spouse
in dark hallows' eve
tomorrow we eat jugged hare,
and autumnal sweet chestnuts

Eduard Schmidt-Zorner – Ireland

Hye Holiday Gathering

Gram prepared paklava and bourma
without a written recipe. Like a newly
hatched bird I'd wait for bits of sweetness
to fall, walnuts covered with cinnamon,
honey mixed with lemon. I stood on a stool
to watch. Before me, at this table Hrpesima and Mariam had
mixed the phyllo and rolled it by hand, but when I was six we
bought phyllo paper-thin sheets from Sevan's Market in
Watertown.

Gram melted butter in the cast iron skillet.
Don't let the butter sizzle-too hot!
She mixed sugar and cinnamon in a bowl for me to add
then got out the heavy rolling pin. I crushed
walnuts beneath its weight. Gram said *be sure
the nuts are ground fine! Grind them again—
still too big.* I pushed the rolling pin hard against
walnuts, then we mixed in sugar and cinnamon.

We took one layer of phyllo at a time,
brushed with melted butter, sprinkled in nuts,
then rolled as quickly as we could.
Finally, using the sharpest blade,
we sliced the fragile rolls and
placed them on the cookie sheet.
Gram's were straight and long,
mine crinkled, like thin fabric.

I have the recipe still, yellow with age,
thin and tattered, like phyllo dough,
filled with handed down memories from those
who sat at this table before me —Shushan, Bedros,
Kevon, Katchador, and Sitanoush cooking
to honor Kharpet and homeland no longer on the map.
Now I'm the old one. When I cook, my

grandmother's voice follows me, step by step

Elaine Reardon – Massachusetts, US

My Grandmother's Kitchen Fifty Years Later

A room dimmed by
distant issues diced and wrecked –
Revealed in recipes
buried in the ashes of memory.

What I remember is this:
oilcloth tossed over the kitchen table,
language in my aunts' assurances,
chopping, stirring, the arrangement

of fried chicken on a platter.
Afterwards
washing dishes with spring water
warmed in the wood stove.

Now the remains are a flavor
flat out and final
welcomings, unwelcomings
wired to what I can no longer taste.

Deborah Purdy – Pennsylvania, US

Pancakes & Steak

cooking pancakes on the griddle
i think of you,
and how i used to serve you
breakfast;
even if i try to will myself not to remember
there are pieces of you
slipping into the periphery of my mind
regardless of what i want—
cannot think of steak
without remembering you liked yours rare,
always called yourself a vampire
but you were more a
werewolf;
and i remember once you said my eyes were
coffee colored
but i am not someone
you can consume—
i am the roots of growing things, the tallest tree,
the life-giving soil;
but you will never devour me.

Linda Crate – Pennsylvania, US

Textbook Dualism: The Lowcountry Boil

who grows red pota-
toes in Illinois? this is
corn country, bruthuh.
a textbook dualism,
this, commonality nil

save for what may be
afforded by some basal
mediator. but
wait, Grandma in Peori-
a gets a Carolina

cookbook, adds shrimp and
sausage to the veggies. the
classic lowcountry
boil sure nullifies the corn/
potato dualism

Johnny Masiulewicz – Florida, US

Family Dinner

It was two hours before dinner service, and bella was closed. Hudson wanted everything dished up, potluck style, on the bar in the next half hour. Denis rolled out crust for curry pies after dumping his paste and coconut milk. Hudson grilled veggie kabobs. The curry was simple: just tofu and carrot and potato. A nice bite. The carrot and potato cooked a bit under to keep the edge crisp. Fried tofu, with a good skin. The aromatics hit the room with a heavy hand. Hudson had already thrown a hotel pan of chicken in the walk-in. It was just the two of them left from brunch. Hudson, the Chef, would be staying on for the next service, while Denis was already off the clock. He dumped his veg into the curry, hit off the burner.

The night crew sporadically appeared, prepped out mise en place. Caitlin, always early, washed her hands, knocked her elbow against Denis' in greeting. Others followed suit, filling the prep counter. They pushed and jostled. Denis kept his shoulders tucked, narrow as he could to not knock into Caitlin as she cleaned squid.

Her paring knife moved quick, a single slice directly under the eye. Fingers extended into the cone, scooping out brain and innards and the pen, which looked thin and translucent like splinters of plastic. A black puddle formed on her cutting board, either ink or vitreous fluid. She tore out the beak at the center of the tentacles, then ripped the skin and fins from the head. Before dumping the calamari into a bowl of water, she ran the flat of her knife over the cone, flushing out the last bits of organ. After each squid, she set down the knife and dipped her hands into another bowl, this one filled with a white wine vinegar. She rubbed her hands with the vinegar. She flicked her fingertips at the bowl before taking up her knife and the next squid.

Denis put the last dollop of curry in dough, pinching it shut and throwing the sheet tray on the center rack. "Bottom oven, four hundred," he said, then repeated--this time shouting to the other side of the kitchen. Pies in the oven, he stepped off line. Finally. He watched those coming up next.

Kebabs finished first. The tomatoes split at the seams of their own skin, which curled back, blackened. Onion slices curled in towards their center. Front of house kept looking for jobs that could get them closer to the bar top, where the platters were set up. Denis watched them scramble for bar preps normally left til the absolute last minute. Supreming grapefruits, juicing anything they could get their hands on. The line cooks laughed when they saw the buzzing front of house. Offered first plate in exchange for beers, which they drank under Hudson's eye--hesitant at first, but with growing confidence when the Chef didn't react.

"Family dinner in ten," Hudson yelled. He reached above sauté station for the jug of cooking wine and poured some into a quart cup. He smiled, lips and teeth stained purple. The smile was awkward, like Hudson was just as confused as they all were that he'd dropped his usual hardass act. Like an act of mercy, available just the once: everyone's mise en place would look like shit. They would cook for themselves, instead. There was no reason for it, nothing that made today different, except that the food--*this* food--was theirs. Their dinner--the chicken and curry pie and the kabobs--none of it was on the menu. Hudson had brought what they needed.

Denis smelled when the curry pies finished cooking, even before he heard the egg timer go off next to him. That stiff, starchy smell so distinct to fresh pastry. They had a good color. Curry oozed out at the edges, where Denis hadn't pinched the dough tight enough.

He carried the tray to the bar top, tossing the oven mitt on a corner of the pan to mark it as hot. Only a couple minutes more, and the main course--chicken tikka masala--followed behind, served straight from the hotel pan next to a pot of rice.

"Who's saying grace?" Hudson said.

"Fuck god. Fuck country. I wanna eat," Caitlin shouted. The words burst out all in a rush, while the other cooks cheered and slammed knife handles against the prep counter. Little divots pockmarked the metal, and the counter sang, hollow and sharp. The rattle of their banging was concussive.

"Good enough," Hudson said. He had to shout to be heard over the noise, and the cooks all went immediately quiet. It was the first time today that Chef had sounded like himself. "Line dishes first."

They ate--front and back of house, both--happy that today was one of the days there was time enough. The pies bit off flakey and hot. They burned their tongues and slurped, anyway. Crumbs hanging off the chin, caught in beards. They'd be in the weeds soon enough. They shoveled masala into their mouths, fast enough to barely taste it before scurrying back to the pots and preps they had abandoned to eat. But came back at the first opportunity, dishing second portions of rice, naked, except for a heavy dab of butter and freshly cracked pepper. They stole lemons from garnish bins, squeezing the stinging juice over kebabs. Yellow rinds piled up next to empty skewers. A massacre of juices, red and the palest yellow, covered the plate. The sharp scent of citrus in the air overwhelmed the pastry smells that still lingered, faint now, around the oven.

Some of these servers would talk, telling their most obnoxious tables about this moment. They would relish their power, however brief, over those that stiffed tips and demanded re-fires. They would hold this moment over the heads of the wealthiest restaurant patrons, proving, if only to themselves, that *they* couldn't be bought.

Neil Davidson – Idaho, US

·borio

             to does not sing,
  _.   plained; put batteries
in your hearing aids, be still,
then listen, he replied

Mark Fleisher – New Mexico, US

Mussels

The shells stuttered against the china.
A flowing river of garlic,
the wet scent oozing down the table:
you hum in oblivious delight
as if Venus rose from the sea foam before you.
Opened and vulnerable,
they were beaten into introversion.
Huddled in their bucket,
fearing the hiss of the pan
and the glug of the chardonnay.
We were eating out to celebrate,
apple juice in a champagne flute
and scolded for elbows on the table.
Yet you crack and splutter each mussel,
sucking them down with a squelch.
You drop them with a plop
into the bloody pool of tomato,
their carcasses still bobbing about.
Without a care for your victims,
you ask for the dessert menu.

Kirsty A Niven – Scotland

BREAKFAST

Breakfast
Crispy bacon
Hash browns, Eggs sunny-side
Favorite people all around me
Family

THE BOIL

The Boil
Served by the sea
Sliced sausage, yellow corn
Orange shrimp, crab, red potatoes
God's gifts

MOM'S DAY

Mom's Day
Shrimp is chilling
Potatoes baking, steak sizzling
Beautiful table set with love
For me

Jackie Anderson – Texas, US

Homecoming

I will bring you up out of the affliction of Egypt...to a land flowing with milk and honey.

—Exodus 3:17
I sift the flour and add the salt
in anticipation of their arrival.
It is good to think of a full house
after so many years empty.
In anticipation of their arrival,
I have robbed the bees and pulled milk from the cow.
After so many years empty,
they will once again be filled with a mother's love.
I have robbed the bees and pulled milk from the cow
that they may taste their childhood once again.
They will once again be filled with a mother's love.
"How delicious!" they will say.
That they may taste their childhood once again,
I have kneaded the bread and watched it rise.
"How delicious!" they will say,
as they spread butter and pour honey on another warm slice.

Jennifer Rood – Oregon, US

Stir

It's mornings like these I rise with the sun. My lashes flutter to the mourning dove's song. The air is still, and I fill my lungs with it. The room is steeped in blue and vibrates in the haze of my waking mind. I'm not alone. My skin unglues from yours as I extend into a shaky stretch and feel something like thousands of happy spiders dancing down my spine. You stir – still lost in sweet slumber. Your skin glows in the dewy sunshine peeking through the shades. Your skin lays tight against your bones. My fingertips trace the length of your arm and I wonder how a being like you was crafted. Dipped in a tub of milk, surely. Sprinkled with cinnamon and cardamom. Bathed and spun like a wick into wax until deemed beautiful and perfect, just as you lay before me now. It's mornings like this I wake to the sun. My lashes flutter to the mourning dove's song. And my heart flutters knowing I wake next to you – lost in sweet slumber and dipped in milk.

Cambria Hines – Iowa, US

Better Than Breakfast

we've skipped breakfast. and the hot water tank
is broken, blocked
with bubbling air. I fill a cup from the kettle
and bring it to the bathroom; brush
and scrub my face, wincing
in the fresh-boiled
heat. then the soap
and then
the razor; a muffled crunching
like butter on toast.
and the cup
steams like fresh tea,
is stirred
just like tea. it's afternoon, I think – no time now
for coffee –
tea; we drink tea
in the afternoon. and last night's hangover
falls away and rinses – something about
losing the scruff
making me feel cleaner
in myself. more smooth, less
poisoned with alcohol. better than breakfast,
if anything
could be better than breakfast. it's 2pm.
I finish, wipe the razor
and rinse out the cup.
in the kitchen
you've been working; preparing
a breakfast – lunch
with a couple
of coffees.

DS Maolalai – Ireland

Pie

He's watching the footie and tucking into a chicken balti pie, and very good it is too, while at home, his wife contemplates the fuchsia in the garden (the Virgin Mary's earrings) and the orchid in the living room (testicle plant) and wonders if crossing them would produce the Virgin Mary's bollocks. Gods, she's bored. She needs an affair, she needs to fuck a vicar in a lift, she needs to be one of the Free French ambulance women, knitting socks while waiting for the next call to the Italian Front.

Hours later, he returns to the Close, full of lager and bonhomie, but the house is dark, the curtains open. He can taste the pie, and it's no longer so good. He fumbles the key in the lock, trips over the draft excluder, reaches out and bends his finger back on the banister, and it fucking hurts. Her fault. No lights. He shouts for her. No reply.

In the kitchen, some floral dissection has been taking place. Fuchsia and orchid parts are in strange configurations. He senses danger, opens drawers and cupboards, finds a tin of sardines and a bottle of Chianti.

She doesn't come home that night, or the next. Nineteen years go by, and he's in the dentist's waiting room and there's a photograph in a magazine, a woman in a white coat, interbreeding plants. He remembers how she would gaze at flowers, and the way he wanted some miracle to happen, that he might be turned into a daffodil or something. He salutes her through his tears. She's made it, she's famous, she's in a magazine. Perhaps she'll come back now. He could murder a chicken balti pie.

Catherine Edmunds – United Kingdom

Edible Flowers

As I bowed my head and closed my eyes during the final prayers for the old woman, all I could see were pansies. My grandmother adored them – she grew them from seeds in window boxes in her kitchen, from tiny pots in her bathroom, and in old Oil of Olay jars in her bedroom, starting them in the thin rays of February light and coaxing them into being when they were ready to be planted in early May when the snows cleared. Her yard was a riot of Johnny Jump-Ups that spread from the flowerbeds and wove themselves into the fabric of the lawn and the cinder path from her back porch to cobwebbed garage. I saw them – the pansies, yellow, blue, red, orange, and all the purple, white, and yellow Johnnies – when I closed my eyes after hours of tending her garden as she watched out her bedroom window. She had grown too frail to work the flower beds and had asked me to come and sort the first flowers of spring from a wild mess into a ribbon of blossoms astride the path.

When I was a child, I would go to stay with her. She would prepare lunches of egg salad sandwiches and tomato jelly served on a bed of lettuce. Scattered in the sandwiches, windfallen over the lettuce, and set in the jelly, were pansies and Johnny Jump-Ups. Each plate she served me was a garden. The first time my lunch blossomed, I was not sure what to do.

My mother had warned me not to eat anything I found outside. My mother grew petunias, and I was told they would make me sick. But after some coaxing, my grandmother persuaded me to taste the blooms. Johnny Jump-Ups are mildly peppery. There is an after taste of something I have never been able to describe properly – not spice or pepper, but something far gentler that speaks to the mouth with a touch of colour, if that's the way to explain it. Pansies are far more emphatic in their taste. They declare themselves with a brisk, slightly bitter presence like endive. I once tasted tiger lily shoots. They taste like pansies.

Taste is the most difficult of all the senses to put to words. Every experience in the mouth has to become a simile, because nothing is like itself; everything is like something else. Language has its limits. There aren't enough words to put in one's mouth, and that has always bothered me as the great deficiency of vocabulary: What lives in the mouth and comes from the mouth is its own silence, its own reticence to know itself. If the hardest thing to imagine is the self, then taste is the hardest thing to describe because it sits on the tongue, masking the words I want to find to explain what I know is there.

But then, there are violets. They, too, appear during the first days of spring. They, too, refuse to be held behind border rows of bricks or petite flower bed fencing. They rise out of the lawn. A violet, unlike the other first flowers of spring, loses its shape, its unique crispness and individuality the moment it is picked. The brevity of a violet is its beauty. In Charlie Chaplin's *Modern Times*, a blind girl sits on the street corner and sells the Little Tramp her violets. Perhaps her tiny hand is frozen, like Mimi in *La Bohème*. The problem with her violets is that their perfume is almost lost the moment they are picked. A bouquet of violets is a small handful of echoes of a time and a place where death rules everything in the world except the life that resists in violets.

On my summer vacation when I was three, I stood in the waves with my grandmother. We sang "Ring Around the Rosy," and I had no idea that "pocket full of posy" consisted of violets to ward off the smell of death from the plague. It would have seemed wrong to explain that to a child, as we laughed and bobbed in the shallows and the waves rolled in and splashed our shoulders. To taste a violet, however, is a very different experience from tasting pansies. Violets do not taste as much as they leave an aroma in the mouth, a lingering sensation that a perfume has entered past the lips and nose and created a beauty that is an expression of taste and scent.

In London, Fortnum and Masons produce chocolates that are flavoured with violets. The cream candies are sweet, aromatic, but the taste is ethereal. On top of each sweet sits a candied violet petal glistening in small crystals of sugar. The taste is sweet, but there is something else, something beneath the sugar that wants to be remembered. I brought my grandmother a box of the violet creams when I visited London on a high school tour. I remember her biting into one, closing her eyes, and saying: "Ah, the taste of springtime."

I had just finished sorting my grandmother's garden when I was called inside the house by my mother. My grandmother had been ill during the final months of the winter. I had thought that the coming of the warm days would give my grandmother her strength again. She had, just days before, sat in the sunlit window of her bedroom, her eyes closed to the warm light on her cheeks.

When I looked up from the yard work and saw her outlined by the drapes, I imagined she was dreaming of pansies. They were almost ready to plant. The flat broad leaves of the violets had already emerged from the thatch of brown grass, and the Johnny Jump-Ups had sent up small, green shoots as the first sign that they were willing to continue with their brief lives. I imagined May giving way to June, thought about what I would plant among her perennials of Sweet William, Delphinium, and Cosmos. I had examined the rose bushes I had cut back in the autumn, and saw delicate green nubs fighting their way through the tops of the stems.

And I tried to remember how rose petals taste when they are candied and flavour the cream chocolates she loved. This year, I thought, I will plant a bush for her. It will be a long-stemmed red rose and its perfume, the delicate scent that hovers over saints whose flesh will not go back to the earth, will help her hold on to life, even as the petals open wider and wider and fall to the ground.

Bruce Meyer – Canada

Beetroots

All tomatoes have rotted and were hanging from the branches
Eggplants and peppers too
And we couldn't make
The mish-mash stew
So we were walking around the vegetable garden like crazy
Stumbling on
Vines, pumpkins and corn stumps
Protruding from the ground like
Breasts of a young woman
Cats were walking behind us too
And meowed
Until father shouted
That he had found two beetroots
They ran off to overgrown
Parsley bed
Waiting until everything finishes calmly.

Naida Mujkic – Bosnia and Herzegovina

Winchell's

Before the 7/11 was open 24/7
Winchell's was where kids
who were too cool to be cool
hung out "at all hours,"
as my Dad would say
in the half derisive/half wistful
tone of one lost to domesticity.

I would see them early/late:
the hungover and the heartbroken
leaning over Styrofoam cups
held by cigarette-adorned fingers
smoke and steam mingling
at the tired, worn faces.

When mom had extra money
and no energy for breakfast
she sent me to Winchell's
to get "a dozen glazed
no more no less," and I
would sometimes add
a bear claw or apple fritter
hastily consumed on the walk home.

Saturdays between cartoons,
I'd see the rich parents
with kids in smart clean uniforms
loading up on sugar before baseball
before basketball before football
before gymnastics before cheerleading.
Kids who never spilled
chocolate milk or cursed, these
laughed at their own jokes
which were never crude or loud.

Nights I walked home
from the skating rink or mall,
high schoolers munched on holes
and sprinkled and iced doughnuts.
If a girl ate a cream filled,
someone seeing the mess,
would pronounce half-accurate prophecies
about the backseat of a Trans Am.
They drank cokes my dad
refused to buy, and went to dentists
to protect and preserve their smiles.

These were the years before
I discovered Hopper, who I now
imagine would have painted
my memories of this place:
the huge glass windows
dank with smoke and fingerprints;
the children hyper focused on the pastel
color of icing and jelly;
the lonely men and women
with no phones to stare into,
only the paper and slowly cooling cup;
and one dirty, long-haired boy
standing outside by his bike,
on his way out of here.

Michael Neal Morris – Texas, US

Pyrrhic Donut Victory

The Guinness record holder
for donut-eating
managed to scarf down
20 donuts in 15 minutes,

but that was 1974, when
waistlines were smaller.

At the breakfast table,
I scoffed, claimed I could eat
at least twice as many.

I was fifteen years old
and weighed 110 pounds.

My parents laughed,
made a bet I couldn't
consume a dozen.

Double allowance
for twelve weeks,
or no allowance at all.
They drove a hard bargain.

I positioned myself
at the kitchen counter
with 12 glazed donuts
lined up in front of me
like shimmering racehorses.

I was permitted
one glass of water,
to wash down the lumps.

The second hand swept to 12,

as I shoveled the deep-fried
globules into my mouth.
My teeth shredded the dough.

The first five donuts
went down easy,
the others not so much.

I began to despise
the flavor of donuts:
a sharp departure
from my usual mindset.

My throat grew heavy
as I trailed the relentless clock,
losing valuable seconds
while I struggled
to catch my breath.

Down by two
at the thirty-second mark:
my parents gleefully
began the countdown.

They were going to save $24,
money that could be used
for beer and cigarettes.

I pushed the last donut
into my mouth, just as the race
ground to its ignominious halt,

but the gummy dough
emerged a couple of seconds later,
dribbled down the front of my shirt,
and finally rested in a slimy puddle

on the kitchen counter.

"You lose!"
my stepfather shouted.

"I knew you couldn't do it.
You can be proud
of yourself, however.
At least you tried."

I was a good sport,
and knew how
to accept defeat
without argument.

To this day, I still hate
the taste of glazed donuts.

Leah Mueller – Washington, US

Long Hot Summer Sundays

Grandma hunches over the hot clatter
of pans in the dim, damp scullery of her roof-leaking,
anciently plumbed, in dire need of a spring-clean,
five-bedroom, one-bathroom Victorian house.

Steam billows in the fly-buzz air as wasps crawl across
gathered early plums and yesterday's barely rinsed
dishes form tottering sculptures on unwiped surfaces.
Grandma does not believe in washing up liquid,

in wasting kettles of boiling water
or in allowing anyone to help.
So, we stay outdoors, clustered amidst
the tended flowers, grown-ups lounged

on rusting sun-beds, dissecting last night's
West End play, or arguing politics.
Six cousin-sisters in swimsuits and plaits
giggle as we race through the sprinkler spray,

beach-balls landing in the colour explosion beds.
The aroma of roasting lamb and rosemary, of potatoes
crisping in the fat, a hint of apricot-sweet stuffing
and undercurrent of overcooking cabbage

seeps out from windows with rotting frames
and mingles with the scent of roses and cut grass,
of honeysuckled summer,
all the smells of childhood.

Sarah Evans – United Kingdom

Marble Hill

Driving,
we push the fog
from the windows to
realize that
we are tumbling
tumbling down scoops
of rocky, sugary gravel roads
sprinkled with snowfall
and pound cake haystacks
we swirl without certainty
through muddy tracks
leaving behind praline tire trails,
swerving clear of
cookie dough speedbumps.
And as we reach the bottom
of this marbled hill,
we roll the milky windows
back up
to resume our
Neapolitan hysteria.

Brian J. Alvarado – New York, US

Hummus

The burden of hummus is
        to be bound to the bland carrier
of bread or cracker
        in the manner of a comedy duo
one with humor
        and one spun straight
or the unyoked couple
        with one golden form
giving aura to the other's
        common obscurity
like a tattoo that requires the savannah
        of a shoulder blade
hummus must be borne
        on a barren canvas.

Jeff Burt – California, US

Mustard and Cress

Somehow, I did not cut the mustard
muster up, was not spicy enough
should have cut it with horseradish
now I'm hoarse with onion allergy
my eyes dripping from the fumes.

I wrest with how to play it. Cool
and sassy with a grinding of fresh
pepper or sad and tormented:
overdone pasta with bland pesto
not enough basil, the garlic raw,
the pine nuts rancid.

I could add cress for the greens—not water-
cress, but salad cress; a British friend
once told me the difference. I am wistful,
wish to play whist to take my mind
off, cut to the chase. Next is the cheese.
Do I want to cut that? I am leaning
into the wind so the rest is behind me.

Stephanie Pressman – California, US

Dreaming While Fasting

At the birth of the world I prayed for birth
and dreamt I sprang a baby. I was sent to a hotel,

unsubtly named the Fair-Mount, where I lurched
utterly lost, as dreams lose us to find others.

While everyone exulted on the mountain top,
fainting and fasting and receiving the word

I climbed the stairs, when I should have taken the lift.
Strange angels asked me if I had reservations.

Wow, do I have reservations.
I entered the pulsing pink-and-white

room womb, where everyone sits, postpartum,
and got my ass a seat at the table.

Then the dream ran out and the whole day raised me like a tent.
I drank milky stars and burnt the roof of my mouth on the delicious sun.

Merridawn Duckler – Oregon, US

Haute Cuisine in Mythology

And when I salted
the Firebird's tail
she flared in indignation,
perhaps,
or merely in chagrin.

The salt glazed her backside
and baked into a hard crust, pinning
her tail feathers together
in a brown-black sheath.

She flew in hopeless circles,
mere inches from the ground,
then fell back to earth,
dizzy.

For her body, I used
brown sugar.

Mikal Trimm – Texas, US

Firsts and Lasts

Everything on death row was firsts and lasts. Grady Wheeler learned that on day one as a guard. His first job as a member of the team was taking Jimbo Turner's last meal order.

"That don't sound too demanding." One of the older Correctional Officers told him. "But it ain't as easy as you think."

Grady hadn't gotten around to learning names, but it was smiles and good will. He stood outside the door of Jimbo's cell. Early the next morning a pair of Correctional Officers would open that door and take him to the execution chamber. They'd walk on either side of him like a pair of secret service agents escorting an important politician. The prison chaplain would bring up the rear, unless the inmate didn't want him. It was one of the few choices left to a condemned man. Last meal was another.

"Hey there Jimbo." Grady's teammates told him first names usually worked best. Faces popped into the square reinforced windows in the steel doors of all the cells.

"Got your last meal all picked out?" He didn't want to say 'last meal' or last anything for that matter, but there was no avoiding it.

"Don't want no cookin'." Jimbo's voice rumbled like the growl of a big dangerous animal.

The team had warned Grady what to expect. A death warrant sat on a condemned man's stomach like a brick. Plenty of the death row inmates were crazy, but few were crazy enough to be hungry. A pair of guards stood down the hallway watching to see how the new boy handled the situation.

41

"Don't be that way, Jimbo." The other guards told Grady to hold out all the hope he could short of telling an outright lie.

"Governor may call."

One of the COs gave him a thumbs up sign. Jimbo Turner was a big man. They'd have a hard time moving him if he didn't want to go. And there'd be reporters looking for a story.

"He usually calls at the last minute."

Men turned quiet on their last day, even loud men like Jimbo. No good rushing them, but waiting it was best to keep the conversation going.

"If he calls, you won't get nothing more till lunch," Grady said.

"Anything you want. If the kitchen can't cook it we'll order out as long as it don't cost over fifteen dollars." Some inmates had mamas who'd cook up chicken and dumplings with biscuits and green bean casserole, but Jimbo's family wasn't in a catering mood.

After a short wait the inmate said, "Ain't had no chili dogs for quite a while."

Faces behind nearby death row windows smiled in agreement.

"No beans in that chili." Once Jimbo settled on a main course his enthusiasm grew.

"Excellent choice," Grady said. "You want fries with that?"

When Jimbo substituted onion rings, the COs watching Grady gave him a double thumbs up. Not bad for his first day on the job.

John Biggs – Oklahoma, US

Prepping Paella
  in memory of MPS

The pans got oiled after the last use,
so I just pull them out, rinse them off.
After shopping, chopping is the big event,
first onions, garlic, leeks, shallots, and parsley,
then tomato, pepper, mushrooms.
I clean the meat of the sea—scallops,
mussels, clams, shrimp, lobster, grouper—
(what have you, as our teacher used to say)
And cut the meat of the land—rabbit,
chicken, pork, chorizo.
I mortar the aromatics, saffron and stuff,
set out the rice while I warm
the oven, the burner, the broth
all this, the way you taught me.
We cooked it together for years
until you disappeared for decades.
When I heard you were dying, I wrote,
but you had died. When I take up
the recipe card, I can still see it in one of your hands,
which you'd chop the air with, saying,
"This is what we're going to do. This"
with all the presence that fueled what you were doing—
furniture making, bread baking, traveling
to Africa, cooking paella, your obituary said,
and said your final mantra was,
"Open your heart," and I hear mine creak.

Diane Kendig – Ohio, US

Burnt Rice

As New Orleans Cajuns,
even in the middle of the forest,
we eat red beans on Mondays.
But not me. I have filled my mouth
with nothing but objections for two days.

You don't tell me we're camping here
in the Mississippi pine-mill woods
because I don't know hunger
nor that as a poor boy you chose
to survive. You never say how many lives
my life is worth as I reject the fish
you catch and fry.

I flick black specks around my plate and protest.
                        Just a little burnt rice.

But burnt rice doesn't have antennae, I cry.
Paw Paw. There. Are. Bugs. In. This. Rice.
A head shake and a smile I struggle to trans-
late like the Couillon French you'll never teach me.
                        You'll learn to eat or die.

Yet, I could find fault in a bowl of cloud.

Shelly Rodrigue – Louisiana, US

What I don't expect

Tenthousanddollarstheygiveyou.Tenthousanddollars. –
                                                 A Raisin in the Sun

Ask students what they would do
if their family suddenly received
windfall like the Youngers. What

they would do. What their mamas
would do. Expect to hear plans
to buy cars, shoes, maybe a house.

Suggest I would save money
for son's college account. Maybe
pay off a bill or book a vacation.

Never occurs to me purchasing food
would be more than one student's answer,

so I scramble eggs, cut cantaloupe,
pour orange juice into paper cups,
plug in crockpot to warm gravy they

ladle over biscuits I rose at *morning-
dark* to bake before school because
it doesn't take much to feed my kids

except to know.

Elizabeth Beck – Kentucky, US

Broken Spanish in the D. R.

Barceló Bávaro, proclaims my wristband,
a free ticket to all the buffets.
I parade through this Punta Cana palace like a queen.
Royalty here in the Cape of the Sugarcane,
I drop $5.00 tips on everyone who serves me.
Dominican desserts line the tables: *Dulce Frío,
Flan, Cocadas, Pudín de Pan*—the Spanish
tasty as ten years ago in high school,
yet *la lengua* has practiced everything since then
but the language it loved.

When I speak to the chef, whose English
is as broken as my Spanish, I order
dos huevos difícil because I remember
the opposite of easy, but not the word for hard.
He smiles and plates two runny eggs. I say
Gracias, never been more grateful.
Later, I try *Donde esta el pollo,* but he hears
¿why is the chicken ugly? instead.
Then, *lo siento* for being so *stupido*.

When he speaks to me in English only,
the bellhop makes me feel better.
So does Tony, my tour guide,
and everyone else except one woman
holding a baby on the dirt road,
who mouths *Agua por favor*,
a desperation I can see
but not understand.

Shelly Rodrigue – Louisiana, US

Tonic

Chester is walking toward us, white towel over arm,
circular tray balancing beverages—Dad's glass, clear cubes,
carbonation, lime; my bright grenadine, stemmed cherry,
ginger ale.
Long Island Sound surrounding: club insignia whips against
its pole.
Boater's air horn blast calls the long slow launch.

He is walking toward us, face puffed,
cockney speech. Places two napkins on the iron table,
then the drinks. My father's face says *Ahhhhh*....
I full-throat my ruby liquid in. Chester laughs.
My father sips his sparkling gin.

Chester is walking away, salty whitecaps splash rocky shore,
sound teal in slanting sun. Motorboats, schooners, yachts.
All the water we could ever want, but my father and I
desire more: we want the kind
you taste, you pour.

Ann Cefola – New York, US

Coleytown, October 1971

The day when Mom was in the hospital
I watched him stare at my lunchbox
and at the cabinets exactly the opposite
of helpless and finally made me
hold out my hand for a couple of dollars
carefully unfolded and told me
to buy my lunch at school today
and I thought of the grey broccoli,
the pink-flecked American chop suey
as I rode the bus and I thought
how I never ate at the cafeteria,
never, the smell of steam and kids;
I always brought bologna on white bread
with just a bit of butter
and two cookies, three carrot sticks
or celery if Mom was mad at me
and I'd sit on the stoop
of the East door, near the first graders'
playground, sometimes cold, or wet,
my temple of solitude
and I wished Mom were home
and he would go back to his job in the city.

Jonathan B Aibel – Massachusetts, US

Mr. Avocado Man

An older man in khakis and a Giants cap sits on a bench
in late afternoon sun
outside Whole Foods on Telegraph Avenue
meticulously stacking
slices of whole wheat bread
then placing one on a napkin

he cuts and positions slivers with his plastic knife
from a luscious avocado
perfectly split, pit left in
setting the pieces like a precious mosaic
then scooping the sandwich with the napkin
pressing the two halves together

over and over he does this
absorbed and content with his handiwork
on his whole wheat canvas
then swallows each in a few voracious bites
taking up the next slice
to begin his avocado dance again

I am mesmerized, envious
picking at my tuna on a hard French roll
having just come from the hospital up the street
refusing to eat in their cafeteria
though there's nothing really wrong with the food
except for me wanting out of the building

my newly-discovered lump gnaws
an unwelcome foreign invader
how did it worm its way
into my soft and sexy right breast

I throw away my half eaten sandwich
closing my eyes as tears pool

sweet memories tingle of fevered nighttime groping
and morning caresses under tangled sheets
I cling to my husband of forty three years

Tell me Mr. Avocado Man
do you come here every day
with your stack of bread and perfect avocado
show me how you make your sandwiches
help me to forget today
and what I must face tomorrow

Joanne Jagoda – California, US

Viands

At the grocery store
I'm hit by the sinking
thought that everything
on the shelves is garbage,
parceled into plastic packages
and made to seem appealing, but
delivering a raging stream of
hormones and preservatives,
not to mention a sky-high
mountain of trash afterwards.
With my perimenopausally-
expanding middle, so sensitive
to extra estrogen it gains inches
even when I eat nothing at all,
I leave with a few organic
radishes and carrots,
bright with the colors of
hope and forgiveness, and a
simple goal: to make
my own damn bagels.

Vivian Wagner – Ohio, US

Tomatoes

In the corner of <u>Best Foods</u>
sit gleaming towers of tomatoes.

Organically grown in fine
"gated communities" far from
toxic sprays, cheap fertilizers.

High above common rabble
produce, many of these tomatoes
will go on to Harvard or Yale.

So what if their price tag is high!
Jammed packed full of antioxidants
they will not linger on the vine.

Feast your eyes upon these healthy
specimens. Note rosy glowing
skins without poisonous additives.

Gourmets: check out organic labels
for vitamin rich food harvested
au natural without preservatives.

These are red-blooded American
tomatoes with no "identity crisis"
about being fruits or vegetables.

Go ahead get fresh, pick one up
and devour a few juicy nibbles.

Joan McNerney – New York, US

Counter Espionage

green onions raid the sweet village
of pineapple, torture the teriyaki,
hold ransom the soft tortilla

olive oil assuaged by political shrewdness
makes pillows of mushrooms
to smother the peppers

lurid purples of cabbage and eggplant
kidnap the purity
of young green spinach

blonde agreements
of batter and butter
meld the pale offspring of eggs

separated yolk and white
now beaten
into a yoked uniformity

garlic spies imbed
in fat congregations
of steak

tongues twist around
the hidden pits of plums
like ancient art stolen from ruins

lips smack syrup as if kissed
by a turncoat of trees,
a traitor of vascular sweetness

knives drum the cutting board
as celery and apples
fall to the side

blenders homogenize berries,
individuals churned
into unformed masses

parmesan shreds
and all of Italy
weeps

Jeff Burt – California, US

For the Love of Chili

At the office the workday winds down, a few of the newer people ask what and where his vacation will be. He slightly shakes and lowers his head as he tidies his desk. Someone comments, that even on the day before his vacation he still doesn't loosen his tie. He's a hard worker, efficient and prepared; stays late, the Boss compliments, he deserves his privacy. Once every year he takes a week-long vacation. For the past 15 years he's worked for the same company; never misses work, never late. No one has found out about his vacation, no pictures, no stories, no hints. Even when he goes out with colleagues or on a date there is something held back.

When he arrives home, he washes all his clothes, puts them neatly in the closet. He unplugs every electrical appliance, then stacks them under the hanging clothes. Only the refrigerator and stove remain functional. The refrigerator is empty, except 2 heads of lettuce. In the middle of the night he goes to a super-market, when there are no people around.

He buys:
2 cans of red kidney beans
1 bottle of cayenne pepper sauce
1 container of oregano
1 small jar of mustard
1 can of tomato paste
1 container of black pepper
1 container of white pepper
1 container of salt
1 block of Colby cheese
1 pound of fresh ground steak
3 eggs
1 loaf of natural whole wheat bread
3 medium Vidalia onions
4 cloves of garlic
1 pack of non-filter cigarettes

3 bottles of 1973 California white wine
1 bottle of 20-year-old sour mash whiskey
and for this year's change: 1 container of peanut oil

He pays with 2-dollar bills.

When he gets home, he puts all the food away. He locks all the doors and windows. Draws down blinds and curtains. He pushes all the furniture up against the doors and walls. The dresser's drawers facing the wall. He drapes red velvet over all the furniture, placing and lighting yellow candles around the room. He strips. He puts his suit into the hamper. He unpacks the white silk suit from the dry-cleaning bags. He hangs it in the kitchen.
He bathes:
1/2 cup mineral oil
hot water
burns frankincense incense
scrubs down with a luffa

He dries and wraps himself in a black cotton robe. He lies down in the middle of the room. For the next 2 days he eats only lettuce and drinks water. On day 3 he changes into the white silk suit. He brings out his special cooking utensils.

He puts the beans in a pot with 1/2 cup of water. He adds 2/3 teaspoon cayenne pepper sauce, 1 1/4 teaspoon oregano, 1 1/2 tablespoon tomato paste, 1 tablespoon mustard, 1/2 teaspoon salt, and 1 teaspoon of white pepper. He turns the burner to simmer. He places the lid on the pot.

He toasts 5 slices whole wheat bread, cuts off and eats the crusts, crumbles it. Mixing together 1/4 teaspoon salt, 1/4 teaspoon black pepper, and 1/2 teaspoon oregano all in a clear glass bowl. He peels 2 cloves garlic, thinly slicing 1 and dicing the other. He pours 1/4 cup white wine into a skillet, he scatters the garlic slices in the wine, then scatters the diced garlic over it all. He sautés it for 3 minutes. He drains the wine and separates the garlic into 2 more or less equal piles. He peels and dices the onions, placing 2 into the skillet with 1/4 cup peanut oil. He sautés them until they are golden brown. He drains the oil and places the sautéed onions in a pile near the garlic. He peels the last 2 cloves of garlic-- slicing 1 and dicing 2. He places them with the uncooked diced onion.

He separates 2 eggs, adding the white to the breadcrumbs. He adds the ground steak, 1/4 teaspoon cayenne pepper sauce, 1/4 teaspoon mustard, the sautéed onions, 1 pile sautéed garlic, and 2 shots of whiskey. He reaches into the bowl vigorously kneading the mixture until it is thoroughly mixed. He flattens the meat into a skillet. He puts the other pile of sautéed garlic into the beans, which he stirs 5 times. He puts the burner for the meat on medium high. He lights a cigarette. When he is done smoking, he flips over all the meat, breaking it into small chunks. He then lights another cigarette, smokes it, takes the meat off the stove and drains the juices.

He takes the cheese and slices it into small slivers 1/2 inch long. He places the cheese next to the cut onions and garlic. He places the meat in with the beans, turning the burner up to medium. He stirs the mixture together, drinks 1 shot whiskey, and smokes 1 cigarette. He uncorks the chilled wine and places it in the middle of the floor letting it breathe.

He turns the burner back down to simmer, stirs the chili, then scoops out 1 bowl full. He grabs 1/2 handful of cut onion, garlic, and cheese and places that on top of the chili in the bowl.
He sits down next to the wine and eats until the whole bowl of chili is gone. He smiles. He belches. It is done. 1 of these years he won't uncover the furniture, he won't plug in the appliances back in, he won't go back to work; he lies down. Some people have dreams bigger than imagination itself. Next year he'll add rice.
Yrik-Max Valentonis – Florida, US

Nightshade

While trying to describe
the colour of a night sky
framed by my office window,

you told me about chilis,
how you grew them
in the window of your flat,

a spot with enough light
to ignite fire in your fingers.
In the family of poisons,

food abounds – potatoes,
tomatoes, and red peppers,
their shapes like houses

sheltering coins of seeds,
sometimes a second fruit,
a fetus twin buried deep

inside a full-grown body,
the brother in a lung,
the nodule of a hidden sister,

an anomalous tumor
or sebaceous cyst –
when cut away, it smiles,

baring eyes and teeth,
aware that after years
it has been unmasked,

its skin a bloody aubergine,
a night sky above the city
ready to hatch seeds

rooted in our language –
words that feed or poison
waiting for the chance to grow.

Bruce Meyer – Canada

Aubergine

I am seduced by your dark purple
heaped in bins at the farmer's market,

envision mounds of Baba Ghanosh
scooped on crisp pita,

or crowning rounds of zucchini.

I anticipate ratatouille,
born sun-drenched in Provence;

meaty eggplant
simmered with yellow squash,

sweet peppers, pear-shaped tomatoes,
all warm from the garden.

Exotic Greece teases my palate,
with layers of lamb-filled moussaka,

slices of eggplant,
bechamel sauce, fine herbs.

I conjure up Zorba's dance,
arms extended, knees bent,

the melody, always the melody,

or Shirley Valentine,
her single table by the sea

inhaling garlic, cinnamon,
hint of cloves, fork aloft.

Sharon Munson – Oregon, US

Friday Afternoon at Mahane Yehuda Marketplace

The *Shuk* in the center of downtown Jerusalem
pulsates with shoppers and vendors.

Merchants offer samples of buttery sesame halvah,
morsels of cinnamon rugelach,
choice bits of Turkish and Kurdish sweets:
baklava, marzipan, rice pudding.

Inside the bustling open-air market
locals and tourists pack lanes
leading to narrow stalls
and a bewildering array of goods—

jars of oil, barrels of olives,
sheep's milk cheeses,
almonds, hundreds of spices,
fresh citrus, oven-baked pita, challah.

In the Iraqi section,
behind falafel stands and juice bars,
old men play backgammon, cards,
slouch at wooden tables,
sip from tiny cups of espresso.

Hasidic Jews in dark three piece suits
crowned by black hats of rabbit fur
shop alongside Sabras
in skimpy jeans and sandals.

Shopkeepers fill cloth bags with fish, beef, fowl,
dates, figs, peppers, potatoes, lamb,
braided breads, almond cakes,
thick white Sabbath candles, sunflowers—
stocking up for Shabbat.

A young, pink-cheeked member
of the Israeli Defense Forces,
Uzi over his right shoulder,
stands guard at the entrance off Jaffa Street

clutching in his suntanned hand
one double dip, pistachio ice cream cone
dusted with sprinkles.

Sharon Munson – Oregon, US

Friday Before Shabbat

Early Friday I rose to the sound
of shifting pots and pans accompanying
my long and playful yawn. I tiptoed

behind the counter watching flour-
dusted hand wrestle *challah* dough
by blue flames of gas-stove burners.

The hum of Moroccan hymns, scent
of garlic and cumin allures passer-by
wishing, *Shabbat Shalom Giveret Varda*.

"Cut the fresh flowers, their scent lingers
long after havdala, and iron father's
shirt. Nu don't stand there, hurry."

"Yalla," my aunt urged, "look at the time,
It's almost *Shabbat*'. I giggled as she
pinned her colorful head-cover firmly

with greasy hands. Together we prepared
the table with the white lace cloth gold-
trimmed china and silver *kiddush* cup

on the eighteen-place dinner table near
the veranda. Father kissed my forehead
before he left with my brothers and uncles

for *minchah*, and I, with my mother,
grandmother, sister, aunts and cousins,
recited the blessing over *Shabbat Lights*,

wished each other *Shabbat Shalom*,
eager to start *Seudat Shabbat* filled with
thanksgiving, song, laughter and spice.

Michael Mahgerefteh – Virginia, US

Two Independence Days

1. Fireworks Day
Oh, it's Nicole.
We were about to call.
You look like you need water.

Sweet fresh raspberries
from the gardens of
both my sisters.
I picked many just this week.

Sweet store bought Hermiston watermelon
brought by my sister-in-law Irene.

Regional sodas and
regional beers.

Don't have too many of those
before driving, my sister says
to her young son
as he grabs another Coors.

Licorice whips and
potato chips.

Where's Shirley? The birthday girl.

I don't know. She arrived late as
usual. Now late as usual, says her mother.

She arrives with
necklaces of red stars,
          of white stars,
          of blue stars,
Mardi-gras beads of patriotism.
July 4, 2007

2. Another July Fourth Barbecue Party
In the kitchen mom pours a local
chardonnay. Pete pours another
Black Velvet whiskey and 7-UP.
My sister drinks from a can of 7-UP
while preparing the couscous and
a simple green salad.

John Wayne Weekend plays
on the living room television.
Pete talks of his hero but he and
my mom teases him *You know
he was gay*, and Big John's
sexual preference would not matter to her
and this was just her teasing Pete.

My nephew Andy is sleeping in his room
before a movie with his buddy
or a girl, who he tells us is just a friend.

My nephew Tom plays a video game
in the office, spare bedroom
and we can hear him yelling.

My brother-in-law Pete barbecue
in their backyard out the kitchen
and office window. He cooks sausage dogs,
peppered steak and
rosemary herbed potatoes. Their border collie,
Roger, offers Pete a wet stick again.

Now smokers break here, the garage,
near kitchen and barbecue,
cooker about half the family and mom,
who quit, criticizes the smokers,
and sometimes their neighbor couple comes

for a smoke and a visit. Soon
my oldest brother and my oldest sister arrive
through the open garage.

July 4, 2010

Nicole Taylor – Oregon, US

Kitchen Witch

On Christmas and Easter Sunday
we are good Catholics
heads bowed in prayer
around a rich table
of family
and old recipes
that have too much
hand-churned butter.
At the altar of the
kitchen stove
women mingle
for gossip and mixed drinks.
We do not acknowledge
the kitchen witches
hung from the ceiling
gathering all the bad spirits
and household dust.
On these days
we are too busy
initiating the youngest
cousin into the art of
grapefruit slicing
to explain that
these traditions
are not superstition,
just added protection
for our own
sacred space.

KB Baltz – Alaska, US

From Apples to Apple Butter

My grandmother's large pot
(the one that was my mother's)
bubbles with white apples
and sugar

Ropes of green and red skins
pile on the counter

We hunch over the kitchen table
words rising and fading
like steam under the hanging light
which brightens
as the day outside darkens

We take turns
mashing apples,
stirring the mixture

Streaks of beige
oxidize to brown inside the pot

Pulp burps and splatters,
our words slow
and deepen

Murmurs and apple scent
float through the kitchen:
the table creaks
the burner clicks
the mash thickens

Hours later pulp
reduces to a thick dark spread
spooned on bread

served with stories spoken,
the best parts repeated.

Sandy Green – Virginia, US

Cucumber Work

vinegars and oils and
salts, acids and alkalis,
bicarbonates, shallow
pyrex glassware bubb-
ling, the blue stove
gas flames and all that
fuckin' cucumber work
like she was practicing
alchemy for dinner

Johnny Masiulewicz – Florida, US

Cake

The woman worked at the counter, image silhouetted in the window. The frizzy hair was tied back and the shape was... Amy? Before she got sick, Chess Pie was her passion, they had always made it together. She was a kid set free in the kitchen, creative side fulfilled. Silently, he held the bowl steady, feeling the scraping beaters. He could smell the lemon juice. When the pan was finished, they played Rochambeau to see who got the beaters, who got the bowl. The image was so real he couldn't help himself. Reaching to take her in his arms...

The space in the bed next to him was empty. Holly never could sleep in. Cinnamon filled his nose as his eyes eased open. Sleep dream to a waking dream. In the month she had been here, this place was home again. Between bad decisions and cancer, she was bald, thin and haggard. He didn't care. Her tattoo said it all, "Here Comes the Sun." The warmth renewed his spirit. Slipping on a robe, he went to the kitchen.

It was a scene from a concert. She was the conductor. Her angelic, bird-like profile shone in the light from the window. She had on one of Amy's old aprons. The pattern matched the artificial daisy she had picked up in thrift store. Bart wasn't one for frills, but the yellow and black petals did contrast nicely against the off-white walls. White blocks of cream cheese sang the melody, honey joining as harmony. A phyllo lined pan lay cooled next to a bowl of crushed nuts, each waiting their turn. Slender hands held the little hand mixer as it strained against the thick batter. It was hard to keep the bowl still enough to work. Reaching either side, he grabbed the edges of the bowl.

"What'cha cookin'?"

Holly jumped. She hadn't heard him come in.

"Baklava Cheesecake for the women's club tomorrow. If you're a good boy, I'll let you have the bowl."

Amy used to say that. Grinning at the memory, he grabbed two cups off the counter.

"Baklava and Cheesecake? The biddies in the building need cheering up?"

"One or two." Holly rinsed the dough off the beaters. "And it's just one dish. Mary Donohue got on my nerves bragging on how much weight she's lost. Not the thing to tell a cancer patient, you know? The least I could do is fatten her up."

They both laughed.

"Amy couldn't stand her either, said she was homewrecker." He placed her cup on the counter "I think it was more her attitude. She'd been a widow so long she'd forgotten basic civility."

"Probably lonely." Holly sighed. She handed Bart a dish to dry. "You do things if your desperate enough."

Holly turned off the mixer and ejected the beaters onto newspaper. Under the wild exterior was a disciplined woman. One step at a time, set up for efficiency. It was one thing Amy hadn't been. The light from the window dimmed slightly.

"Ooh, scratch my back."

Purring as his nails went across her skin, she went back to primping the pan. Batter cascaded into the bottom of the crust. Another layer of pastry followed with honey and chopped nuts. Finally, everything met her satisfaction. The pan went into the oven with a clunk.

Her eyes crinkled as she loosened the knots on the apron and let it drop.

"Here comes the sun."

The batter coated spoon slid into his mouth, followed by her lips. Arms and hands found their places.

"Happy, now?"

"Mmm…" He closed his eyes. "You taste better than the cake."

"I taste like Chemo." she snorted, pushing him away.

He kissed down the scarred body.

"Better than nothing at all"

Vanilla, cinnamon and honey mixed as they pressed against the counter. Sunlight reflected on wrinkled flesh and it was good. There was no hurry, just call, response, and flow. Release came.

He pulled a chair and watched as she cleaned the kitchen. Unlike Amy, she preferred to do this alone. Sipping from his cup, he watched the frailty come back. "Amy would tell me 'to give anything less than your best was to sacrifice the gift.' The same spirit is within you."

Holly picked at a mint plant in the window, "My only good boyfriend used to say that." Her voice got softer with the memory. "I wish I had listened. It would have saved a lot of grief."

"I'm just amazed I have as much energy as I do."

She placed her hand on his.

"What should we call us? Are we a couple? I mean after the last month, I'm really not sure…"

Bart pulled her into his lap, fingers tracing the inked sun.

"Two people God wanted to heal."

The words were comfort. Comfort for their lives and healing for the spirit. They basked in them for a long time until the question came.

"And when it is all over?"
"I'll cry when it happens. Right now, I'm grateful. You should be, too. " Helping her to her feet, the smile became bigger. "Let's get a shower."

Christopher Mitchell – Georgia, US

All the Way to That Way

the onions
fry up beautiful
down in the pan
with the steak
and mushrooms.
half as many
baby tomatoes
settle in a separate pot
(she likes them,
I don't)
and there's a bottle of red wine
warming by the fryers.
we're stinking up the evening here
and everything smells delicious.

I clear the table while she does cooking
and talk to her a little from the door,
then cross the room and look out the window.
the sky is clear
and white as a glass of water
and it goes up from here
and all the way to that way
then around again
and the same
but backwards.
the room is filled with sounds
and cooking smells
and shines
with the fresh light
of outside
walking in.

over the houses in the distance
a football stadium
rises like red flowers.

behind me
the frying gets quieter
as the pans are moved off the heat.
a second later
there's breath on my neck
and gentle hands

DS Maolalai – Ireland

Dysphagia

At half past seven it is time to take
our seats. Dinner is ready, and good food
should never go to waste. We try to make
light conversation to improve my mood
but find the effort awkward. You consume
the salmon, squash, and baked potato much
more quickly than I do. Throughout the room
long shadows dance in firelight as I clutch
a paper napkin, soon committed to
the trash along with remnants of our meal.
Tonight we fail to bicker over who
does not clean up. False strife has no appeal.
"The fish was really good," you kindly note.
I still can feel a bone within my throat.

Jane Blanchard – Georgia, US

Cast Iron

I do not own a measuring cup. I have no idea how much sugar it takes
to sweeten us again. How much salt to pour into the wound, so you regret
our cleaving. This marriage, how baking soda cannot replace powder; how neither of us is a baker. How
we forgot to eat the anniversary topper.

Maybe you're right: I undomesticate everything I touch; dye
the silver of my hair blood red. Was I too feral at 4am?
Did you think I was kidding when I told you?

love isn't binding agent. It's trusting the dough to rise while you work
on the filling. It's how you treat the accidental burn, then the blistering.
How you ration disappointment. A wedding dress yellows over time.

You married cast iron; you married the plates we will break; the decanter
we drink from. Not cake, not layers of frosting, but garden, but the sweet meats. Yes, the tongue, liver; the casing that holds what we devour together.

Natalie Illum – Washington, US

Capital Nourishment

a big mistake that must've weighed a ton,
served medium-well with Worcestershire sear.
that i myself would too soon be well done,
a joke i chased down heartily with beer.

i hesitate, brought back to my first date—
the awkward lull before the mutual gorge,
the cliff from which we hang ourselves like bait,
above the valley we ourselves did forge.

the acid reflux fizzle calmed in time,
gave way to remnant skillet sizzle drone.
remained the rim unmelted was the rime,
i left no tendon hanging from the bone.

i savored this, the taste of close demise,
i only wish I'd asked for shoestring fries.

Brian J. Alvarado – New York, US

Pasta in the Nude

There are certain things which
should never be tried by stoners.
Top of the list: making pesto.
Try the pluck and snap of basil
branches without weeping inside
from all of the vast exfoliations.
Try finding the pine nuts,
rifling pantries, on hands and knees,
head to the floorboards.
It feels cooler down there.
Or the climb of stools as if
the barest burned out bulb
ignited by the pull chain
were some essential spice.
What about walnuts? OK then.
Walnut pesto. But it chokes
the blender. There used to be
a long handled grilling fork
outside by the grill. You find it
and in spite of the rust
stir the green pulpy mass.
When the blades unlock,
metal on metal on glass,
the blender carafe shatters.
Is life ruined? Smoke another.
Reflect deeply. All you have to do
is gather every shard, fit pieces
back to make sure the sauce
isn't lethal. That is you,
picking, gathering, fingers bleeding.
Never mind the pesto--why add
meaningless layers of meaning
to everything in your life?
So, you sit down to plates of bald,
overdone noodles you forgot

in the explosion of everything.
Your stoned lover not too
stoned to say, needs salt.

Barrett Warner – South Carolina, US

A Brief Blinding

At dinner I accidentally flung
sriracha into my eye.
Just before impact, I saw
the length of cabbage I failed
to cut enough fine turn
into comic miniature seesaw,
my fork coming down too hard
and the sauce sent flying
the only direction it could go:
the face of a dumbass.

Then burning blackness
and sudden fear the eyelid
would remain shut
at least as long as it took
to dissolve the vile jelly.

Of course, it was dramatic
for only the few minutes
I managed to not trip
on the way to the bathroom--
though I imagined doing so,
adding a cracked skull
to my tragi-comic routine.

Quick thinking spouse,
patient with her old monster,
helped to flush the flaming face
and within minutes we (I lightly
gasping) were back on the couch
watching the latest *Blue Bloods*
(paused during the fracas)
and finishing a fairly quiet dinner.

Michael Neal Morris – Texas, US

Dreaming of William Carlos Williams at a Vietnamese Restaurant

I have devoured
the entire bowl
of tofu vermicelli,
which made
my belly swell
like a thundercloud.

I don't need
forgiveness.
Nobody else
was going to eat it
except me.

The rice noodles
dripped with
salty broth,
and the spicy
peanuts exploded
between my teeth
like perfect firecrackers.

Leah Mueller – Washington, US

At the Chinese Restaurant

While we wait for takeout, let me read
your fortune. We'll sip tea until the server returns,
watch the toddler behind us toss noodles.
Everyone we know is just a little bit
      splattered.

The day after tomorrow is as far from now
      as next year,
your receding hairline an Etch-a-Sketch erasing
our Kung Pao, Chow Fun, your Great Wall.

Let's remember to leave extra coins on the table—
tell a story with our nickels and dimes
about somebody's future.

Keli Osborne – Oregon, US

Random Recipes:
Curried Pterodactyl with Fried Bananas

Ingredients ---
1 pterodactyl
5 pounds curry
30 bananas

You will need ---
1 turkey baster
1 blow torch
5 fuel tanks for blow torch
1 mallet
1 back up mallet (if you are a messy cook like me)
1 hacksaw

Directions ---
Bam! Burn! Bite!

Yrik-Max Valentonis – Florida, US

Nuts

It said on the bag of nuts
May contain nuts.
It did not contain nuts.
I had eaten the nuts.

Joe Williams – United Kingdom

```
        J       J       J
        O       O       O
        L       L       L
        T       T       T
        I       I       I
        N       N       N
        G       G       G
```

```
            coffee coffee coffee coffee coffee
         when the weary body begins to atrophy
      one needs to find the remedy to give the holistic jolt
this is the                                    supreme
beverage of                                    the working
      class hero in all capacities and forms, the wonderful
        libation that raises the spirit, the numinous burst of the
          air, rich steam, the goodness, the lift of the pheromones
            the rush of dopamine through cortices and      cornices
              of the psyche, crevices of the wrinkles and   saturated
               with adrenaline rushes, side effects are the   perpetual
                reddening of the eyes as the blackening in   the beaker
               undergoes a transmutation that dissolves    fatigue
              whitening from the milk, lightening the big load
            with some folks experiencing crashes from
           the overload of a speedy serum, anecdote
          we pass to friends, an art of media
           laced with extra foam
            and cream
```

Jack M. Freedman – New York, US

Ode to Margarine

I have something to say—
And it's only a little thing

But in the face of French cuisine,
corn on the cob, and toffee

And for ghee and for toast
I say: fuck you margarine.

Why are you 99¢ a pound
while butter is $5?

Ginger Lee Thomason – Utah, US

Affront to a Madeleine

Godzilla wears a red beret
his sister bought in France.
He looks through catalogs
for stripy shirts, practices
diffident shrugs and smoke
rings.

Godzilla would have
a lover but hasn't a spouse.
He can't read poems to sons
and daughters—he has none.
His tepid coffee tastes like
Dubuque or Bakersfield,
Merde.
        He stabs the shell
        on his plate.

Keli Osborn – Oregon, US

How to Cook a Moon

Blend milk & flour,
vanilla & egg, a dollop
of cooking oil for good
measure. Beat until the
color resembles Laughing
Cow cheese. Heat crepe

pan to the temperature
of a heatwave in Alaska.
(That's pretty hot.)
Dribble a bit of batter
on the pan. Cook fast
& hard, feed to the dog.

(The first one is always
a little punky.) Dribble
again, rotate the pan
to shape the batter into
a full moon: rotund,
bulbous, sphered. Cook

until the edges gold, until
you make out the image
of its crescent on the
horizon, until you can
take your first steps
on its surface.

Kersten Christianson – Alaska. US

The Sanctity of Bread

It's always been mine,
this sacred practice,
this moment of purity and stillness
wrists-deep in the folds of my own creation.
The ritualistic movements bring me to church,
to an altar dusted with flour, abundant with hope and purpose.

There are no promises in bread,
no holy vows, no guarantees.
In bread, there is only desire,
there is only ambition,
there is only the dream of what can be.
It is a ruthless art, one that has as much potential
to disappoint as it does to please.

This creature of yeast and flour and anticipation
owes you nothing.
This creature, to whom you've given life,
is a thankless trickster,
is Discordia incarnate.
With endless opportunities to lead you astray,
the prayer for victory is nearly futile.

And yet, we approach this altar,
our sanctified house of worship,
and are nearly brought to our knees
in plentiful veneration.

In the words of Dumas,
we, unworthy parishioners,
wait and hope.

And so, like the bakers before me,
the weary yet sanguine pioneers,
I bend in faithful devotion

and hope for the promise
of joy and stillness that
a simple loaf of bread can bring.

Lauren Cutrone – New Jersey, US

Ode To A Kitchen In Connecticut
　　—with an apology to Wallace Stevens

I
Among twenty loaves of bread,
The only moving thing
Was the poet's harmonium.

II
I was of three minds,
Like the unbraided strands
Of a challah.

III
The recipe whirled
Through the kitchen
Like a blackbird's wing.
It was unreadable
Behind the scrim
Of equivalences and substitutions.

IV
A poet and a reader
Are one.
A poet and a reader and a baguette
Are one.

V
I do not know which to prefer,
The precarious music
Of kneaded dough,
Or the transparence of almond icing.

VI
Winter cracked the brittle crust.
The focaccia collapsed in the oven.
Was it rancid flour

Or the poet's inscrutable hands?

VII
O gourmands of literature,

Why do you imagine golden loaves?
Do you not see my inkwell
Filled with bright crayon?

VIII
I know the flat river
Reflecting the wilderness of stars.
But I know too
That leavening
Is part of what I know.

IX
When I hurled the chapati
Down the hillside,
It inscribed the sky
With maxims of coriander seed.

X
Acknowledgements scribbled
On a thin sheet of paper:
Solitude ripened
Like an Anjou pear.

XI
Once, fear pierced him
In that he mistook a loaf of bread
for the shadow of a blackbird.

XII
The biscuit is rising.
The poet must be writing.

XIII
It was Connecticut all afternoon.
The brioche was baking
And it was going to bake.
The scent of yeast lingers
In the cedar limbs.

Suellen Wedmore – Massachusetts, US

Butter Me Up

I like butter, I want it
but the butter's too hard
too soft, too salted, too French.

I like butter, I want it
but you've spread it too far
you've spread it too near.

I like butter, I want it
but cultured please
and saltier. And more French.

Whoa – that's way too much.
I said, that's –
oh, wow.

No, definitely don't stop.
Spread it near
spread it far,

butter me up, butter me down
salted or un, this side or that
French or non.

James Gering – Australia

Morning Prayer

Into a heavy, tri-layered sauté pan

Sprinkle a thin layer of crushed Big Jim
  you purchased from a trading post
  while on pilgrimage to the Santuario
  de Chimayo to seek blessing
  from a faith like, but not,
  your own. Also,
  kosher salt.

Ignite the burner
  on your gas stove which burns only
  natural gas formed by the slow
  decomposition
  of the wild vegetarian
  sea beasts of the Paleozoic era.

Place the pan over a medium high flame.
  The fire will vaporize pepper oils,
  elements drawn from the ground
  blessed by the Virgin.
  When the first of these oils
  meets you,
  the olfactory epithelium
  will ignite the memory of her
  beside the stream flowing in Chimayo.

Drop into the center of the pan a dollop of room temperature grease
  which you have reserved from previous

  ecstatic bacon experiences.
  As the recollected excess
  melts, mammal and plant
  will bloom into a vermillion flower
  and release
  an inflorescence of thought, word, and deed
  rushing through sage brush and piñon.
  Once the wind has liquefied,

Add to the pepper and salt and grease one clove of garlic
  minced to a paste using the method
  you learned from a once royal chef
  who, rejoicing in his Michelin star,
  now trades bon mots with other
  culinary retirees and their children
  while demonstrating basic food preparation
  to supporters of your local public
  broadcasting station. When
  the garlic soul rises unto the Lord,
  glorious in his saints,

Introduce to the pan three eggs
  laid by happy hens roaming the fallow
  barley fields watched by young Sister Rita,
  friend of St. Francis and youngest member
  of an elderly convent located
  some miles out of town.
  The eggs, collected by fellow members
  of the community supported farm,
  having gently been washed and delivered,
  should have been briskly whisked, the albumen,
  chalazae, and yolk well-mixed into one substance.

Allow the eggs to marry
        the pepper, garlic, and grease.
        The ceremony will take, perhaps,
        longer than you believe
        but shorter than it feels.

Move the mixture about the pan
        using a bamboo spatula
        ordered at a party at which you were
        the only male guest, a spectacle,
        as though your wife had trained a chimpanzee
        to use sign language and where the ladies
        spoke to you slowly and in short
        sentences.

Remove the eggs from the pan
        before you think they are done.
        Residual heat will continue
        to coagulate proteins
        for an impressively long time.
        The conversion of egg into food
        will be worked out in fear and trembling,
        coming to completion upon
        the ceramic plate glazed white
        where, with chives and extra salt to taste,
        breakfast waits to ascend on stainless fork.

Todd C Truffin – North Carolina, US

How to Eat an Omelette

Give thanks to chickens
Set a place mat on the table
Look at the exotic angel plant that sits atop the middle of the table, add water if needed
Set down fork and napkins
Pour a hot cup of coffee in your favorite mug
Read two poems after the first bite
Let the cherry tomatoes fall out of the omelette and eat after you have a good amount of goat cheese on your tongue
Read the last poem in the book you've invited for breakfast
Preferably an anthology of sorts
Take another bite, you should still have a bit over half an omelette left
Drink coffee while you cut another piece of the egg, spread ingredients over it generously
Eat it all up, drink your coffee, and write a poem

Edward Vidaurre – Texas, US

untitled senryu

grandma
makes everything better
pinch of salt

new cookbook
in my arsenal
bibliophile

priceless
I inherit
mom's recipe box

let's bake cookies
the price of
a smile

making an exotic dish
with new spices
blind date

Dr. Ronald K Craig – Ohio, US

Ode To My Cast Iron Frying Pan

Now I will praise you, my 30-year-old cast iron fry pan,
For you have been a cherished tool for half my lifetime,
For you do not discriminate tenderloin from ground chuck,
For your service is uncompromised, even in the outdoors,
    over a log fire,
For you maintain a resonant hue and symmetry,
For you go from stove top to oven without complaint,
For you can fry an oyster and come out of it
    with a shiny face,
For you can move into a new day
    with only a swish of soap and the swipe of a paper towel,
For you offer my blood a jolt of iron,
For owning you, the cost invested was less than a Christmas turkey,
For you permeate my kitchen with the scent of garlic braised in olive oil,
For you offer up a crisp slice of bacon,
For in your care a lamb chop glows and swells with gravy,
For you strengthen biceps and triceps as I carry you from hook to stove,
For you delight in summer,
    offering up generous servings of fried, herb-scented chicken,
For you delight in winter,
    offering up corn bread and savory beef stew,
For you delight in autumn,
    offering up acorn squash braised in butter with brown sugar,
For you delight in spring,
    offering up almonds and pecans, toasted for salads,
For you outperform Teflon
    (which succumbed many years ago to scratch and
    peel),
For you are resilience

    smothered in liver and onions,
    the backbone of a blueberry cobbler,
     and a platform for the best tamale pie with braised skirt
                                                         steak
                    and brown butter cornbread
                                                  in the world.

Suellen Wedmore – Massachusetts

To Grandmother's Fallout Shelter We Go

My grandparents built a new home in 1952. At that time my grandfather decided to add a fallout shelter in their basement. This was quite a radical decision as no one we knew had one then, or ever for that matter. My grandmother was skeptical and feared it was a waste of money. Fallout shelters are enclosed spaces designed to protect occupants from radioactive debris. There was much concern in the fifties over nuclear bombs. School children were taught to *duck and cover* under their desks, in case of attacks. They were also taken into school basements for scary bomb drills.

I remember my father whispering about this special room to my mother. It gave the subject an air of mystery. My grandfather felt this information shouldn't be public knowledge. He was a well-known painter and wallpaper hanger and didn't want his clients knowing that his new house had a fallout shelter. He said if his family ever needed to use it, he didn't want to turn people away, and there was barely enough room for his large family, if that.

For many years my grandparents hosted Thanksgiving in their new basement for our entire extended family. The basement had a sink, refrigerator, and stove for baking the turkey, a wood burning fireplace, large tables, furniture, and room for many guests. Plus, their main kitchen upstairs had an oven for cooking a large second turkey. Moist dark and white turkey meat, creamy mashed potatoes with gravy, and wonderful, spicy stuffing! Is there any better meal?

My aunts stayed overnight with their parents to help with everything, and it was a major family event. My mother was known for her date nut layer cake with penuche frosting. The fact that all the grownups loved those ugly dates amazed her children. I was a card-carrying member of this group. Mom soaked the oversized, wrinkly, raisin-like blobs in boiling water to soften. How disgusting. We'd try to talk her into making her famous fudge brownies or a Dutch apple crumb pie. This juicy dessert with cinnamon and brown sugar crunchy crumbles on top was mouth-watering. Add a scoop of vanilla ice cream on top, forget-about-it!

Nope, Mom wanted to bring another date nut cake. People had specifically asked. She couldn't disappoint any of them. We had to admit her frosting was straight from heaven and worth a quick swipe from the side of the cake, where it was always extra thick! If you were careful you could find little pieces of dateless cake crumbs with fudgy tan icing. We considered the mince meat pies our aunt brought even worse than date nut cake. We never went near those monstrosities. They contained something strange Mom called mixed meat suet. Please! Were we feeding birds or humans?

The conversations around our tables were always varied; football games were very popular with the men. Our city had a parade the day after Thanksgiving when Santa came to town and stopped at a popular department store. That was always a favorite topic with the women. Another was the most coveted toy of the season, which the kids chimed in on. Usually, there was a last-minute, dramatic shortage when no one could find them in the stores. Yet, strangely enough, someone knew someone who could find one for usually twice the cost.

I remember the Thanksgiving when I first peeked into the strange little room on the other side of the basement; it's not a clear memory. This was many years after it had been built and was basically an abandoned closet. One cousin whispered to me in hushed tones that the room was a *fallout shelter!* My immediate reaction to the cramped, windowless area was wondering what would people do in there for a long period of time? I think the walls were made of cinder blocks or cement, but I couldn't say for sure. I remember a couple shelves on the wall held canned peaches and maybe a board game or two.

Fallout shelters were no longer in the news, and most of the eeriness of the room had vanished.

When the popular television show, *The Twilight Zone*, broadcast a controversial episode in 1961, it rekindled the timely debate of the ethical dilemma of private fallout shelters. It could be very dangerous choosing which of your friends and family would be allowed to enter. Not a choice I'd ever want to make.

Christine Collier – New York, US

Mama's Silver
    – for Carol

Lift the lid of the handsome cherry chest, roll the hidden hinges.
Fine sterling rests in the slots where it has been stacked

for decades – knives, dinner forks, soup spoons, serving pieces.
Rub a finger over the velvety lining that soothes slight scratches

in bright metal. What does the soft luster of neatly ordered
handles and blades reflect? A shapely bride, middle child

of an earnest family, traveling by train one January across the South
to a military camp in Louisiana to marry her grinning airman,

revved up on the runway to war, who'd wrangled an overnight pass;
the festive meal welcoming a son home from the polio hospital;

an ailing grandfather's poignant birthday celebration; the first
visit with Mama and Daddy of a certain boyfriend, grinning himself,

head in his own clouds with love. Each piece knows a story,
each tine, each small smooth bowl, each edge muted too long

in a stepmother's hutch. Now, all are in a daughter's grateful hands
and can again do their natural work: spear a generous bite

of Company Mushroom Chicken, scoop a section of Men-Like-It Salad, spread butter on Mema's Spoon Rolls, piping right out of the oven.

Larry Pike – Kentucky, US

Blessed Meals During Cursed Times

Holding the same Biblical urge
To end barbarity's scourge,
My antebellum ancestors
Wanted a rescuer to emerge.

Left beside their regrets,
They sought manna for their palates.
And there was a seasoned trove
All over some ebony mama's stove.

Provided you had their edibles,
Existence felt palatable.
Punches were munched apart.
Mamas fried, sautéed or baked,
And sent another ache astray.

Their recipes sent servitude's hurts
Past tyranny's outskirts.
Mamas' food helped sorrow get hauled
And it allowed love to be installed.

Watching gladness protrude,
Mamas gave nutrition to various broods.
Considering the fortifiers they served,
I hope them mamas heard,
I hope them mamas heard
Thank you.

Bob McNeil – New York, US

Things They Never Said I'd Miss

At times, I think of all I lost in leaving:
buskers—their string and brass tunes
carried from Causeway Blvd to Café
du Monde, music textured like
étouffée, a dish I can't get
from anywhere else on earth, or
gumbo that my grandma made;
hand grenades on Bourbon Street—
intoxication at 9 am like it's normal;
jazz bands leading protests and parades—
Krewes of Carnival. They never said I'd miss
Louisiana's four seasons: crawfish, football,
Mardi Gras, and hurricane; the
Natchez steaming down the Mississippi;
Oz—the land of drag queens, sweet as
pralines, best show this side of the French
Quarter; Monday-slow-cooked
red beans and rice; even the dead
second line for weddings and funerals;
Tchopitoulas. They never said I'd miss
underneath Claiborne Bridge;
Voodoo tours in the Vieux Carré;
Winn-Dixie and Circle Food Store;
Xs on Marie Laveau's grave.
Y'all, I miss yaka mein and
Zatarain's seasoning on everything.

Shelly Rodrigue – Louisiana, US

Tamales Mean You've Arrived

No joke to abuelas who spend
days wrapping corn husks. Only
best teachers deserve this gift.

Elizabeth Beck – Kentucky, US

Lunch Lady

I imagine her strong. I imagine her weak. This lunch lady with Spanish rolling off her tongue like rivers.

The radio in the kitchen stays on evangelists that call their flock. Shepherds going after lost sheep with radio waves.

Who is coming to save her? Is anyone looking for her?

One day, I overheard her say the word cancer on the phone, her Spanish unable to cover it from my ears. Or, did I imagine this?

We talk food and family. She eats salads. Is a picky eater. Her young daughter teaches in Korea and took a recent trip to India.

There are grandchildren here in New York City. She spends time
with them and friends from church on the weekends.

I imagine a group of grandmothers walking the streets, the weight of the world chipping from their backs.

They are in the sun. I cannot tell if they are walking toward it or away from it. But it is shining.

The lunch lady has a life outside of the school's kitchen. She has family. She has friends. She has learned to survive.

Elvis Alves – New York, US

During the Butchering

A woman waits in a long line to buy fish calculating
how much she needs to serve 24 and how many bones.
She watches the man scoop carp out of the tank.
They flop on the block until he hits them behind the eyes.
Their guts pile in a bucket beneath the counter.

At the back of the store behind a door of wired glass
a man clutches a chicken by the neck, slits
its throat, severs neck from body, the limp head
on a wooden surface. He loses hold and the body
scurried across the cement floor, wings flapping.

The woman's daughter watches the man chase
it, sees more headless hens run wild over fields
with policemen in pursuit pointing their guns, hunters
with rifles slung and a wolf tied to a long pole.

A Maasai youth ochred and wrapped in purple blankets
his foreskin split, carries an olive firestick. The bitterness
of acacia smoke lingers on his skin.

The daughter watches, detached, remembering
the feel of chicken skin loose on the necks
of young hens before she tossed them into soup with long pointed
carrots, tufts of celery, and chunks of parsnip aromatic as wine.

After her mother's death she carries her, year after year,
to the fish market, all the heads ready to use, but the eyes
milky, the scent fishy rather than briny. And as she skins
filets, pulls the bones left by shoddy knife work,

the Maasai boy starts out across the Serengeti with
his fellows armed with bow and arrow, pointed sticks

to fend off lions, seeking sunbird, barbet, turaco
to brighten his headdress. She feels herself leave

with him. Brightening her headdress with the whitened
bones lifted from the broth. Seeking the lilac-breasted roller.

Stephanie Pressman – California, US

Black Meat Chef

White Buffalo Tongue Woman flew
over white snow-prairie,
flew to white-capped mountains,
into white-skinned aspen woods,
into the square, white-washed tepee
of the white man with bloody hands,
hands bloody with the blood of black meat
soaked in cow's milk, dredged in white,
bleached flour & sautéed in an iron skillet
with white onions over flameless fire
& reeking of a herd of death & her own
silence, silence for more than a century,
silence until now, when his white tongue
speaks this white memory before dawn.

Karla Linn Merrifield – New York, US

How to Slow Boil Your Twin's Heart for a Hearty Munch

On a particularly sunny Wednesday afternoon, the Twin rushes home like a wretched shadow of his former self and hands his heart to you.

'Here, take it. I don't want it anymore.'

You receive the heart smeared with blood and grime on the palm of your hand, the way one might receive a delicate chicken. The organ was still beating.

'Why? What's the matter?'

'I don't want to talk about it. Just take it.' The twin retires on the sofa like a war-torn general.

'But it makes no sense. Your heart should belong to you only. In any case, what I am supposed to do with it?'

'Burn it. Throw it away. Slow-boil it, for all I care. I'm done with it.'

He falters towards the bookshelf and picks up a copy of 'The Outsider' by Camus. You just stand there dumbstruck, having no clue what to do with a beating heart.

You almost throw it away, but then decide against it. Maybe it's better to slow boil it after all. 'A peppery broth of the Twin's heart'-there's a certain flavor in the phrase.

You've always been an innovative cook and a voracious reader for that matter. The Twin had his mind over football and motorcycle repair.

You wash the heart of the grime and blood. You put the heart inside a pot with some water and light up the stove.

'Camus was a filthy bastard!' the Twin proclaims and throws away the copy. He was never much of a reader.

From inside the pot, you could still hear the faint lub-dub under the hissing sound of the boiling water.

'Gosh, that's a strong heart. Wonder why he wants to get rid of it'-you think.

The Twin has picked up a copy of 'A Moveable Feast' by Hemingway.

You start chopping onions and garlic.

The Twin rushes through the pages.

'Hemingway was just a drunk guy who is profoundly over-hyped'. He throws away the book.

You sigh. You've seen the pattern enough times to recognize. It's a downward spiral. He'll end up settling for Dostoyevsky and feel miserable for no particular reason.

Inside the pot, the vegetables flow in a serene manner centering the heart, quite like ballet dancers. The Twin is rummaging through the bookshelf.

'Isn't there a single decent book in your collection??'

You toss fish sauce and pepper into the pot. The broth is almost done. Sure enough, the Twin has picked up a torn copy of 'Crime and Punishment'. You gracefully scoop up the heart along with some broth and put it in a soup bowl.

117

'Do you wanna taste of it?'

The Twin doesn't reply. He just sits there with his hands over his temple. The book lies open on his lap.

You put a spoonful of heart inside your mouth. The visions rush in like a torrent. Ah, now you remember. It was raining. You were inside a cafe. She was wearing a red dress. You start to feel miserable for no particular reason.

Hiya Mukherjee – India

Acquired Tastes

Sweet is the gift of sunlight
on snowy mornings in midwinter,
the garden spread like caster sugar,
the harvest table gilded in honey,
the carpet in our hallway raspberry –
you mix my senses to your tastes
so apples remind me of your laughter.

Sour is an evening when snow falls,
when the wind puckers our faces
with the cold surprise of limes,
cheeks pinched at the medicine of time:
for what cures us of our coughs
tastes worldly with its weary news.

We have learned to swallow bitterness,
times when even the best-laid plans
vanished on the tips of our tongues
and made us want to spit out life
in search of something else to swallow;
for hardship is an acquired taste;
it passes but leaves a memory of fear.

Salty is knowledge we've had to learn,
the tang of sweat, the bite of sorrow,
the knife that every mouth must feel,
the sea, the spray of heavy waves on shore,
heavenly in teardrops on your naked arms
as I dried you and we cried together.

But the meat of life, the savory we know,
the test of truth as we test each other,
regardless of sunlight or rough weather –
that taste is why we share our hearts,
the fine, warm course lived hour by hour –

the evening meal that sustains each day:
come share with me this feast of life.

Bruce Meyer – Canada

Cold Carrot Curry

Remnants of last night's carrot curry,
our weekly vegetarian meal,
sit in the square glass bowl
on the bottom shelf of our refrigerator.
I lift the silicone preserver,
sniffing and inspecting
swirls of browned cumin and ginger
playing about the edges of
carrot disks and chick peas.
Congealed bright yellow oil,
encircles, framing the carrot disks,
Envelopes chick peas on top.
The aroma of ginger tempts my
hunger and I pull it out.
Reheat? Stove-top or microwave?
Tradition or modern solution
for this ancient recipe?
Yet, that congealed fat
calls to my half-piece of naan
like a rich butter.
In current form the bowl
is a paisley symphony, an
edible silken sari.
Instead of heating to
rejoin flavors, my naan
scoops a portion to my mouth
where taste buds and my psyche
revel in each aspect of yesterday's glory,
separate flavors, textures come
together in the heat of my mouth
to reform the dish, as is,
straight from refrigerator.
Sighing, I find resurrecting this cold version
superior even to last night's warm delight.
I reach for a glass of pomegranate juice

to toast my discovery that carrot curry is a dish best served cold.

Joan Leotta – North Carolina, US

How To Grow Basil

It starts with a three-tiered cutting of basil, passing delicately over the farm stand table, from his gloved hands to her ungloved ones. "Put this in water and let me know when it starts to grow roots."

So, she fills a cleaned-out, 12-ounce jam jar with tap water and places the basil in her bedroom window where it gets full sun every day. When she wakes, it's to the sight of the thin leaves, backlit and luminous, their verdant, sun-hot scent filling her nose. Every morning unlocks the memory of him holding the leaves out to her, telling her in a low voice what makes *this* basil different. And her inhale, so deep the smell of the soil on his glove intermingles.

Roots, spindly and spiky, pierce through the stem. That week she carries the glass jar to the market in both hands to show him the beginnings of growth. "When they're an inch or two long, it's time to plant them," he says, holding the glass jar at eye level. "Remember to keep the water up. Thai basil is not like sweet basil. It's thirstier."

Every morning and every night she keeps her eye on it. And when she's away during the day, she leaves her mind with it. Her coworkers tell her she seems a little distracted. She replies that she's fine, thinking instead of how the tips of the bottom leaves have started to brown and curl. They fall, dying, into the water. But a new spiral of budding leaves emerges from the top. "It's okay," he says, plucking the brown ones from the surface, "it's the new sprouts that matter anyway."

When the roots reach the bottom of the jar, he holds out his hand and offers right then, in the middle of the market, to take her to a pottery store a few blocks away. "Our first date, if you want it." And he says it so shyly that she *wants* so much, takes his hand and lets herself be led to a store with a seedling for a sign, no overhead lights. Just the cool, spring sunshine through the window.

She runs her hands over the fine-grain surface of each pot, deliberating and drawing out the moment. She settles on a classic terra cotta the color of his skin, with a body that tapers down into a matching base. He pays, and back outside, they weave through the market to the compost stand. He hands over two, smooth single dollar bills for a bag of soil, and they go back to her place to re-plant the basil.

And it grows. The plant moves out of her bedroom and into the kitchen, and he moves into both spaces. For a time, she wakes up to the smell of eggs, oily and salty, and the brown-sweet scent of caramelizing onions. He makes better use of her closet-sized kitchen than she ever did. And though she thinks she's being sneaky, watching him without a word and breathing silently, he turns around to her, holding spoon over hand. "Taste this, tell me what you think."
Weeks pass, the plant grows bigger, and new stems shoot up from the soil. He buys compost from the market to sprinkle around the plant base, and she waters it faithfully, every morning before work. Her coworkers lean in over her lunch, sniffing hungrily. They smile and tell her that she looks so happy. She grins and shares the recipe he taught her.

They make it through a sweltering summer this way, with the windows open so that a tepid breeze can blow through the apartment. The scent of basil (and soy sauce and sesame oil, rice noodles softened and then fried with egg) spills out onto the fire escape, never lingering. He brings in new ingredients on the weekends, sets them down on the wooden counter and dissects them with a chef's knife. Here, the edible leaves. There, the tough, woody stem that's better used ground up and dissolved into hot soups. The peels can be eaten; crisp them in the oven to make chips. The seeds should be discarded; even baked and dried they are bitter, and sugar does nothing to save them.

The basil outgrows two more pots by the time it gets too cold to leave the windows open. When he cooks, she can smell it at the bottom of the stairs, and though her stomach rumbles with craving, it's roiling with dread. The sourness of the fish bone broth, the vinegar sauce, condenses in the closed space and seeps into the fibers. The more delicious the meal, the more potent its odors. Her coworkers lean away from her, the floral scent of her perfume not quite covering the memory of last night's dinner.

She eats what he makes, hungrily, tastes the basil from the windowsill before biting into a whole peppercorn, accidentally forgotten in the broth. Her tongue shrivels, her mouth burns. He pours her a glass of milk to help her wash out the taste, and it's with the ghostly memory of the pepper still lingering that she says, "Can you cook something normal tomorrow?"

They argue. *What is normal?* And the dinner grows cold between them. The indulgent dream ends, a final sip of rice wine tossed into the sink. He walks out, not bothering to button his coat. The day after, she uproots the basil and lets the pot fall to the floor.

Caroliena Cabada – Iowa, US

The Rages of Garlic is Love

Garlic, you poser,
snowy-hearted non-participant,
lying languid in the pantry
like a chilly-shouldered bimbo next to old onion.

I blow your cover,
peel bulb apart,
your cloves spring
thick and waxy as eagle's talons.

In the kitchen,
I cut and crush your bite-size payloads;
you, in conspiracy
as your true, hot nature's revealed.

Through the press you spread a powerful new altruism,
your odor broadcasts communal intentions
to make a fragrant, pungent neighborhood of a pot of beans,
intoxicate through dozens of incisions in salmon fillet.

You begin delicious missions quietly
to smooth sticky blood,
silence bee and wasp stings,
lull black plague to sleep,

Stimulate appetites.
You radiate through pots of chicken soup,
add glow to spoonfuls of mesquite honey
to ward off coughs.

Your release from fragile skin
wreaks pale but potent havoc,
building momentum to clear arteries,
clear throats, clear out crowds with one mighty, sulfuric
breath,

That thwarts post-dinner Valentines
and after-midnight vampires alike,
your righteous anger subsides when two
partake of you at the same meal.

Like a tuning fork that matches
the pitch of a guitar string,
garlic gourmands vibrate on the same note, smell sweet,
the food of love not meant to be eaten alone.

Cynthia Gallaher – Illinois, US

Oregano Has Left the Restaurant

smells like Canele's pizzeria
on Chicago's northwest side

where minty, oily, nose-tickling
aromas of oregano once hovered,

along with odd-named members
of the real "Pink Ladies" girl gang,

Tootie, Zorine and Twitch,

pizza in the 1950s was big news,
maybe bigger than Elvis,

oregano? Not so much,
but after more than a half-century,

its covert ways as antidote
for food poisoning, parasites

now grow. who'd know?
this era when antibiotics reach,

grapple, then throw hands up
in surrender to bacterial resisters.

no match for the green-panted upstart
who can start a rumble

with e. coli, salmonella, candida,
trichomonas, even high school warts!

showing the toughest crowd that oregano's
even more powerful than the loaded revolver

old man Canale kept behind his pizza counter.

Cynthia Gallaher – Illinois, US

Night Kitchen

We wave and butterfly,

our hands, our shrimp,
our eyes

caught up in love triangles.

Nothing feels completely broken
down.

We trim and scrap.

We scrape our knees and snappers.
The spiders do

as they please until they
freeze

above pistachio gelato.

Chef smokes and makes
decisions

on a flight of stairs
that leads

to the street and turnip greens
past their prime.

Most of the diners have gone home.

Those still here decode the menu
with shiny, black eyes.

Glen Armstrong – Michigan, US

Savour

Since I stopped working in kitchens
I feel liberated in taking my time
I move slowly
I dance through the art of a meal
I enjoy the solo sound
Of my own peaceful voice

Since I stopped working in kitchens
I feel liberated by my lazy knife strokes
I lick the spoon
I eat finger food with a knife and fork
I rebel against the memories of control
Of the anger-garnished faces
Framing my former kitchen nightmares

Since I stopped working in kitchens
I stopped working in my own kitchen
I remembered how to savour
The soft, aromatic experience
The joy of the art
That comes before a meal

Sarah Jane Justice – Australia

Ham and Legs

Mary Jo's a genius. The other day I was having rubbery ham and eggs with her mother. "Tell your intelligent daughter she has beautiful knees," I offered. Then the earth shook. Everything went south (including my lunch almost). I crushed her mother's corsage.

Been at this funky hotel ever since. Apparently on a clear day you can see Catalina from the rooftop Jacuzzi. I've seen nothing but concrete and overcast. "Hans!" I yell for the Miracle Whip blond bush boy. Abled by a pair of bone white thighs, here he comes now zigzagging between the porcelain paving tiles. "I'll have my breakfast in the Jacuzzi!" I tell him.

He holds up a pair of secateurs. "But I work in landscaping," he says, over the whirring jets.

A little wink and a shrug. "All the same to me."

After he makes an orderly pile for my things, I shyly step in. Then breakfast comes (great because I'm starving): gravelly ham and eggs. The surface of the plate is agitated by the jets. I lose a tooth in the eggs.

I call for the bush boy.

In several, long loping strides, he materializes through the vapor.

"What is it?" he asks.

"Not so good, Hans!"

"Not my problem," he says.

He leaves and after having the wildest dreams concerning Mary Jo, I wake up unrefreshed. A white grand piano, I am seeing it now for the first time.

"Hans?" He stands before me like he's never left. Indeed he probably hasn't. "Is that a Steinway?"

He nods.

"Play me something. Anything," I say, and hand him a one-hundred dollar note (the one with George Washington's face on it).

The momentum shifts.

What happens next is seismic, vexatious.

My world, smashing open like a gravelly egg.

Shane Moritz – Maryland, US

Rhonda Threw a Reuben On

As rain held for another hour

Miranda's Cornered Café
Stood empty in Lynchburg's last strip,
Before highway and Blue Ridge woods

Each of its sixteen tables
Covered with brown vinyl
Boasting white, square menus
Devotedly placed to form plastic Crosses

A blessing for tuna on rye and compressed with cheese---
A benediction for grandly boiled eggs
And pickle spears served on the side

And Miranda calls for Rhonda to throw a Reuben on:
With a thick slather of Thousand Island on rye
Pushing never to be an Island short
Lest she desecrate
Kulakofsky of Omaha's gastronomic masterpiece

A winking nod to Reuben himself,
Cursed for his love of Bilhah:
Poor Reuben loved one so vanquished
A heart adrift on some Island for want of soothing hands

Or perhaps here is a great nod to Marjorie Rambeau
Sitting alone in Reuben's Deli in the City
After nightly bowing to strangers
Deep in the Proscenium
What amazing worlds a sandwich might rouse

So with mounds of beef piled
And capped twice by the needed Kraut
And slices of Swiss ensuring the Edifice's holiness

Rhonda adds golden fries,
Though a chilling storm will come.

Rhonda pitches her work
Under a fevered lamp—
Behold, a Sandwich!

Les Epstein – Virginia, US

The Legacy of Jose Padilla

In the L.A. winter of 2004, Blanca worked the counter at Jack in the Box. A short, stout, coffee-colored woman, she didn't like me, for no reason I'd ever given, though I often suspected I looked too Caucasian for her despite my Sicilian flesh and fluent Spanish. She'd bristle at my arrival, and when I'd hand over money, my eyes would look to meet hers. She never made eye contact, which naturally drew my gaze to the scars over her left eye, the ones made in Life's piercing shop.

Then came *the* night. I ordered. She delivered. And it wasn't the food's smell, or the taste, or the texture. It was how long she'd been out of sight. I dumped everything in the trash the moment her back was turned.

Audrey, the cashier, was a tall, lovely girl from New Zealand. She liked everyone, a true Golden Retriever of human beings. She watched, mouth agape.

"Why did you *do* that?"

I sat back down, sipped the iced tea I'd poured.

"Because of Jose Padilla."

Audrey screwed up her face. "Who's Jose Padilla?"

"In 1989, I was food poisoned at Burger King. The cook had poisoned eighty-six other people. All white."

"What? OK. So wait... alright, how did they catch him?"

"He poisoned a cop's wife."

Audrey looked toward Blanca. She was handing bags thru the drive-up window, using short, curt words toward a manicured woman in a silver Mercedes SUV.

"You're being ridiculous," said Audrey.

"Everyone's always thought so."

I returned from New York the next week. Audrey greeted me with a big, friendly smile. I ordered my usual, took my receipt and relaxed.

"So what's new?"

"Well…"

She described the detectives. Two days earlier they'd visited Selena, the pretty daytime manager whose life's purpose is sticking to the rules.

"They took a copy of the store's video surveillance, then they came back and arrested Blanca. She'd been getting people sick. You don't wanna know how. What was that guy's name..?"

"Padilla."

Audrey looked down. "That's… it was her cousin."

I nodded. There was no need for 'told you so.' Some lessons you never forget. One of them is understanding why there are some people who won't look you in the eye.

Matt McGee – California, US

Salt and Vinegar

Rrripp, pppfffff

bags are opened
and nitrogen gas

esssssssssssscapes

no longer forced
into foil wrap
servitude

crinkle, crinkle

hands plunge in
to grab

crunchy, crackling,

munchy, lip-smacking
barbeque, ranch
ketchup and ripple,
sour cream, onion,
chive and dill pickle
potato chips

chomping, champing

chewing and spewing
crispy crumbs
in all directions
with gusto
but

gagggggggging

at the acrid bite of
salt and vinegar –
a flavor I will
never relish.

Fern G. Z. Carr – Canada

Crispy, Crunchy, Gone

Don't look for the potato chips,
   I ate them,
Ate them all, every bless-ed
   Son of a spud
Ate them with roast beef,
   Red and rare
Partnered with the yellow
   Of garlic pinon mustard
Spread on multigrain rounds
   Red and yellow -- colors
Of New Mexico's flag
   And banners unfurled
In Spain and Sicily, Macedonia
   And Montenegro,
By ancient enemies
China and Vietnam,
In Kyrgzstan, too

Yes, I ate the potato chips,
     Low-salt baked chips
 You bought four days ago
   Or maybe two days
Sixty percent less salt,
Thank goodness,
For taste receptors of
   My tongue
Leap at briny sensations,
   Seasoned temptations

Yes, I ate the potato chips,
   Not all at once,
But over a few days
   Each fresh chip crisp
As a newly printed sawbuck
   Crunchy like crinkly paper

Yes, I ate them all, and
  Yes, I remembered
To put a rubber band
  Around the bag
So, the chips stayed
  Fresh and crispy and crunchy

Mark Fleisher – New Mexico, US

The Invitation

Come and fill,
Mottled meats over piles of roughage;
Flows through, pours over – offers nothing.
We fill and fill –
Piles of fruit,
Already dead. Already rotting.
The vines have grown for decades;
We take the bounty,
We tie the vines –
Twisting them to our will of forced production;
Fill me and mine own.
Bellies distended from eating and eating,
Stomachs stretched.
It's no matter.
For we know that man is never full,
Never satiated, never satisfied with enough –
Come and fill.
The table has been made ready.

Justin Hunter – Missouri, US

First, the Slaughter

First, the slaughter;
Carcass hung to dry.
Days to weeks pass – whatever you like
Halved with a chainsaw
Anus to neck
Quartered at the 13th rib;
Meat Saw – Thin bladed knife.
Gambrel and chains; stab and raise high
Legs off a the hip,
Leave the bone.
Cut muscle to the belly
Fill the bucket with fat to be rendered;
Slash down alone the backbone,
Cut ribs. Grind the pieces of meat that fall.
Saw shoulder – remove the leg;
Next the neck
Steaks dropped into brine
Wrapped. Frozen. Shipped.
A hundred bloodied hands;
Gore to the shoulders;
Sweat and cold and stench.

Today I went to the market.
Today I bought a steak.

Justin Hunter – Missouri, US

How to Fry a Daughter

Her fried chicken was legendary. It always was. She brined in in buttermilk. Seasoned it with herbs and salt and pepper. And then, perfectly coated and fried. Eggs. Flour. Eggs again. Flour again. Always juicy and crunchy. It put the Colonel to shame every time.

"You get a job? Still running around like a chicken with your head cut off?" She asked.
I knew what chickens with their heads cut off looked like as they ran around the fenced-in chicken coop. It was if they had almost escaped but then became dinner anyway.

I knew there would be no fried chicken breast if I didn't answer her. Or somehow explain. Or even just lie. She needed me to confess.

She balanced a crunchy, juicy chicken breast over my plate. And over my head.

"I killed it. Plucked it. Soaked it in buttermilk. Seasoned it with my secret recipe of spices and herbs. Fried it to crunchy, not burned. How long have you looked for a job?"

It was if she was a fifties housewife in a television commercial, chicken-hawking fried chicken but only for good children. I imagined her chasing the chicken. And the chicken wishing it could fly but being stuck on the ground. She caught chickens with her bare hands and then laid them bare on a tree stump to cut off their heads. Sometimes, she didn't even bother with the chicken head cutting cleaver. When she didn't have enough time, she would just snap their necks with one of her thick fist grasps. I always wondered if that method was more humane, less struggle, less pain. Either way, there were always white feathers and white chicken bones glinting under blood streaks left behind from her fried chicken carnage prep.

"Breast or wing?" She asked again as I was ordering my dinner.

Hungry, I mumbled "breast" and then followed up with "I'm working at KFC."

They weren't the right words. I knew they weren't. I had never made good fried chicken at her house. Or mine. The chicken always turned out bland and limp, no crunchy exterior. A dangerous hint of pink if I wasn't careful in the cooking process. She tried once to teach me how to kill chickens in the yard because grocery store chicken was subpar. I chased the chicken like we were both in a Saturday morning cartoon, silly themed music playing in the background. There were no chicken feet leaving the ground that Wednesday, mine or the poultry version. I failed. And she still fed me. After she snapped the scrawny chicken necks of Sophie and Caroline and Mark III.

This time, I wondered if I would eat. I had betrayed her. I was frying chicken that started frozen, pink breasts and legs and wings on Styrofoam trays. Flour with corporate spice flecks the only hint of flavor.

And yet a crunchy thud of chicken landed on my brown gas station plate. Next to potatoes that were lumpy because she hadn't killed them, only dug them out of the ground. The first bite was touched with the guilt recipe we both always carried, unspoken words on a blurred recipe card she carried from her mother. She flashed a sturdy white-toothed smile, wiping still-greasy hands on the apron that barely wrapped around her, its ties nearly cutting her in half.

I ate and then left the table leaving a plate of chicken bones behind. I caught a glint of my own picked-clean bones, now blindingly white. I walked, a flightless bird with my feet on the ground.

Mother picked up her axe to bring in tomorrow's dinner.

Amy Barnes – Tennessee, US

The Mistress of Staggering
for those with chronic pain or mobility issues

Separate your actions into parts.
Don't attempt multi-tasking.
Being on the stagger may require a seat,
it may require a rest whilst kneeling
before cupboards and fishing out a bowl.
It will require the bowl to be placed above you
before you haul yourself back up.

Here's how to stagger a crumble: apples
peeled and chopped today, then in the fridge
with lemon juice over-night. Rub butter
into flour tomorrow with the sugar. Set oven
at one-eighty for roughly an hour.
Done!
Millionaire's shortbread is in three layers,

it's made for staggering:
boil a tin of condensed milk for two hours,
turning every half hour and topping up the water.
That's your caramel, a bit soft but will do.
Next day make the shortbread. Rest.
When it's cool, layer on the caramel.
Melt chocolate and drizzle, today or tomorrow,

no-one's counting days except you.
There's a cheat: caramel
can be bought in cans already done.
But supermarkets may not have it,
and on such occasions
it's good to know
staggering is an option.

Cath Nichols – United Kingdom

Recipe

So as not to disappear she grew bigger
and bigger, battled her own weight,
the forced march of calories;
units of heat cancelling units of love.

In this photo, however, she's only a portion,
exalted and magnified, covered in praise
sauce, She's the plate they passed,
the candle they lit instead of chewed

and the bread they broke. At the table she memorized
tattoos like recipes written on the wrists,
where they fiercely argued with death over
what called for a pinch, what a fistful, of salt.

Merridawn Duckler – Oregon, US

Folie a Deux

Over two-hundred-seventy dollars' worth of groceries. For one September weekend. One couple. Thirteen plastic bags' worth. Shoved into Toyota trunk. Spillover in back seat? Bulging-bag, frozen-chocolate babies, secured with belts. Fried, buttery, and/or cheesy children? Safe in said trunk.

Calvert and LorrieAnn rushed their sedentary selves onto worn front seats. As if synchronized, both turned to face the back. Both leaned over, maniacally searched for victual treasure.

Must have taken twenty seconds — tops — to locate diet goodies, but for Cal and Lorrie they might have gone spelunking through an endless pitch-black cave.

"Cal," Lorrie spoke without looking up, "where are they? Do you think we left them behind?"

Cal shook one plastic bag, tamped down his smile. "Relax, Li'l Lore. I have a few boxes here."

Lorrie despised Cal's "Li'l" nickname for her, especially as the term hadn't even fit (ha, ha) fourteen months ago, when they'd first met — when she'd been sixty pounds lighter.

The currently two-hundred-and-five-pound, dark blonde did not want to remember how *nearly slim* she'd been the day they'd met. Nor did Lorrie want rage coloring her face as she recalled the roughly five-hundred-pound Cal selfie he unashamedly thrust between her face and her half-pound cheeseburger during their first meal together. He'd also described gruesomely detailed steps of the gastric bypass he'd undergone about two years before they'd met.

At the time — at their first dinner out — she'd graciously listened, thought: *how brave of him to share this private trauma.*

Lorrie now realized that Cal as much as told her his former self was *still* a large-looming possibility. He had warned her, but she'd been speaking the language of romance ever since that afternoon fourteen months ago, had willed herself not to be bilingual until, perhaps, today.

No, Lorrie again chose not to think. She needed fudgsicles to numb tongue, throat, brain. Needed an avalanche to bury… Cal? Herself? Both?

During this getaway weekend Cal didn't need to fear being alone with his fiancée. The Spartan quality of his parents' upstate New York bungalow would likely keep Lorrie uncomfortable both days.

Though very early September it was icy-cold upstate, indoors and out. The bungalow's water was still turned off. Furniture was sparse, amenities nonexistent: a small piece that doubled as dining and writing table; two hard-backed, uncushioned chairs; one twin bed in each of the two bedrooms. No rugs. No television. No books. Yellowing magazines going back two decades or three. Two blankets, two pillows.

Unlikely even Lorrie would demand sex in this environment.

The next day, if all went as he'd planned for the night before — night into dawn shoveling down store-bought fried chicken; mac and cheese; and family-sized tubs of French vanilla pudding — Cal and Lorrie would awaken in separate, cold-as-Cal's-heart bedrooms, with carbohydrate hangovers they hadn't experienced since the first time they'd slept and eaten together.

Lorrie had wanted a weekend trip for the two of them, alone. That's what Cal would give her — emphasis on "alone." His laughter chilled his bones, rattled his cavernous heart.

It woke Lorrie from choco-fudge quiescence. She wiped her mouth and chin: brown stickiness adhered to her pudgy palms. Looked at her pants, straining at the thighs: still-cool fudgsicle droplets dotted dark denim. And at her feet, on Toyota floor? Piles of wrappers frantically ripped, intermingled with gnawed sticks. Many sticks: more than could fit in one, two, or three frozen dessert containers.
At her left, slumped over five empty fudgsicle boxes, Cal in his dark brown "puffy" jacket. Dark brown, he'd advised her, showed few stains. Puffy "accentuated" his "football-player physique."

"O.K., time to get these groceries to the bungalow." Lorrie tapped his forearm. "Come on, you'll sleep it off inside." No response. She started to pick up dessert detritus from the floor. Stopped when Cal nearly fell on top of her.

It was bitter outside, and the Toyota's windows were closed, but families in the parking lot clearly heard Lorrie's penetrating screams.

Iris N Schwartz – New York, US

Bones

Thick, savoury smells of Thanksgiving turkey, stuffing. Tsimmes: stewing
carrots, prunes, pineapple and honey. Sour-sweet, like the memories that
come today. My mother's kugel – not particularly patriotic – not something
the pilgrims would have eaten. But that's the beauty of Thanksgiving:
history amended as necessary.

I remember the lean days – my lean days – when I would eat nothing at the
table – a nibble or two for the sake of peace, perhaps. And to escape, I would
do the clean-up, eating what was left on the plates to feed my salience, my
wisdom, fighting the urge for invisibility. Striving for indentation at any sign
of rondure. Bones with only the slightest remains of meat.

And somehow she espied me. Somehow, she discerned that she could see
my reflection in the china cabinet; if the angle was just right, she could see
my method of cleaning up. Eating everyone else's unwanteds, taking in the
unwanted to reinforce my own sense of unwantedness. The invisible vying
for visibility made by reflection and degrees. And here I thought I was getting
away with something, unknowing that visibility was not as elusive as I
believed... or invisibility.

She only told me this years later, when the china cabinet was long gone and
my need for invisibility had become less urgent, less viable. Or less visible.

A revised memory demands refraction,
a new brand of mirroring…
the intentional gaze remanded,
its angles, softened, sour-sweet

Jaclyn Piudik – Canada

What We Put in our Mouth Matters

I'm a vagitarian
For those you who need that broken down
It means that I'm a lesbian AND a vegetarian
Hence vag—itarian
Basically, I eat pussy and lentils with equal abandon

You are what you eat
And what we put in our mouth matters

I grew up in a small-town white-bred recipe of boy meets girl eats meat and potatoes mundaneness
My sexual choices pre-packaged like my food
In my small-minded hometown
Bagels were considered exotic
I mean Jews invented those after all
Any cheese besides Kraft slices or cheddar was eyed with deep suspicion
Like my bosom best friendships with other girls
Which struck the wary grown-ups as excessively exuberant
And so I grew thin
Becoming invisible
Like the alternatives I could not see
Until my does-not-belongness was confirmed with a one-way ticket to university
Where I discovered a veritable smorgasbord of spice, choice, flavour and abundance

Indian cuisine, in particular, was a revelation
Here was an entire culture of millions sustaining themselves cruelty-free
Foods mixed together in a crazy mishmash of flavours
So different from the compartmentalized plates of youth
where peas did not mix with the roast beef which did not mix with the potatoes
Each eaten in an orderly turn

Salt and pepper their only meager extravagance

When I tried Indian food
I learned things could go together
That seemed incongruous
Like how yogurt raita on rice was scrumptious
And when I tried an Indian lover
I discovered the same
Like how girl on girl was delectable
My taste buds blossomed and I learned to appreciate simultaneous contradictory flavours
Like dark and earthy meeting light and bright in a thoughtful pairing
Crunchy and smooth co-mingling or chewy and melty in one sweet mouthful
My romantic horizons followed suit
When I first came out
I resisted dating butch women
Thinking as my culture encouraged
Why date a woman who looks and/or acts like a man?
The answer, my friends, is simultaneous, contradictory flavour
Boobs and bravado is a potent flavour combo

And yet
Both my lesbianism and my vegetarianism
Remain perceived by most people as lack
It's framed in their minds as giving up something good
But that's not how it has tasted to me
Both discoveries opened up whole new worlds of sensation
They're not lack but novel abundance

Look,
If mom's over-cooked, mushy, bland side dish veggies were really how I ate
If the long-nailed, hair-tossing, prissy girl-on-girl scissoring of porn was really how I fucked

Yeah, I'd be deep-throating me some kielbasa too
But those are mainstream myths
There is no deficit here
I mean really, where's the deficit?
You can strap on a dick but not boobs
Just sayin'

My lesbianism
Like my vegetarianism
Is as much about ethics as it is about pleasure
They say that every dollar is a vote
And this may be hard to swallow
For those you who do...swallow...
But so is every orgasm
And personally, I don't thrill to patriarchy

I mean you know what they say
"Four boobs are better than two"
Ok so I'm the only one who says that
But it's true!
At least for me
And it might not be for you
And that's cool but just consider

They say put your money where your mouth is
I say put your pussy where your politics are

I mean if you're gonna eat a chicken
You might want to consider how it's been treated
And if you're gonna date a guy
You might want to consider how he's been treating others
Is your relationship free-range and organic?

And yes, I'm comparing men to meat
And maybe that's offensive
Or maybe it's just a refreshing goddamned change
All I'm saying is

Be a thoughtful shopper

I mean I think pleasure should be
A grand adventure into the unknown
Glittering with uncertain thrills
So experiment
Be an intrepid erotic explorer
Try durian, kumquat, kombucha, chia
Place different bits on different bits
In startlingly fresh ways

Look,
I'm not really trying to recruit you
To my vagitarian team
Just to inspire you to expand your palate
And consider its consequences
You are what you eat
So what we put in our mouths matters.

Raven Sky – Canada

Porridge

steeping a sticky saucepan I watch
small raindrops falling
on a leafy garden

weighted with sorrow the buckwheat porridge
steaming from the morning bowl
with my nightmare

on a gluten-free diet everything tastes like cardboard
I'm trying to sweeten my day
with sugar-free jam

Agnieszka Filipek - Ireland

Eating Oatmeal

Oat groats, rolled, cut, pulverized to porridge,
food of my childhood and now,
most mornings. Revered by my mother as
her mother's Depression staple—my father's
family's served PA Dutch mush—who served it
the times we had time for its stewing,
that grain given, as Johnson said, to English horses
and Scottish men. "But *such* horses,
such men," replied the Laird.

She convinced my father of this breakfast,
and though she's dead ten years, he has it
each morning; in his dementia, maintaining
mobility, cheer, continence, health,
and a deep belief in oatmeal,

which I believe in since my doctor
looked at my numbers, and said,
"I guess it does work," so I went further,
to its cakes, its haggis, it laverbread burgers,
but mostly to what North Americans call oatmeal,
meaning morning hot cereal steaming now
in my pan due to land in my bowl
and stick with me.

Diane Kendig – Ohio, US

Weekly

Summer arrived as daybreak
And putted rhyme on my uncle's lips
Which seem he has been programmed to sing
Because 'It's summertime' was breakfast of our ears every cock crow
This rhyme, clouded his mind so much
And rained out note on every door post
'Saying; it's summertime
The living is easy
The beer is cold
And seafood restaurants are throwing open their doors
No better way to consume ocean's fruits
Than with a paper plate on your lap
The wind in your hair
And creaky floorboards beneath your feet'
This note, clothed us with deep interest
And we embraced the summer in seafood restaurant
And the summer left us with nothing
But delicious seafood memory
Which awake love for seafood restaurant visitation weekly?

Temitope Ogunsina – Nigeria

Oyster

I am the fisherman
who plucked you from your bed,
an oyster in its shell,
closed up against the world.

There is darkness in you,
a single grain of sand
that broke in long ago
and burrowed deep inside.

I do not know whether
you took that intruder
and sculpted it, shaped it
into a perfect pearl.

Or chose to ignore it,
denied its existence,
allowed it to remain
untreated, infected.

Let me open your cage
and take a look inside,
to see what you have made
of the blemish you've borne.

And if there is no pearl,
I will devour your flesh,
discard the empty shell,
and dive for another.

Joe Williams – United Kingdom

A Memsahib Learns to Cook

She was now a memsahib, the youngest in the battalion.

The service wife, she was told, must institute a homelike atmosphere for her man and her progeny. "She must adjust herself to the community as she finds it."

The community as she found it was too neighbourly. The men were too curious, the women full of advice. Most of it the unsolicited kind. But that's how things rolled; she was in the army now.

She had never learned to cook. Reputations were made and unmade in the kitchen, standards were high. So, late in the evenings, she made her Captain teach her skills. They started with chai, moving up the food chain one recipe at a time.

She was glued to YouTube, her girlfriends sent her Pins. Sergeant Blimp's Drumsticks and General Harrumph's Wings. Major Grey's Chicken and Cavalier's Grill. Soon, with the blessings of Nigella, she was a domestic goddess too.

Her household grew in proportion to her prowess in the kitchen. Sunday to Sunday, trips were made to the regiment store; an herb garden bloomed on her windowsill. Her travels added to her pantry. Rajma from Jammu, kesar from Kashmir. Coffee from Coorg, Nilgiri tea. Two pressure cookers, one charcoal grill, and a food processor later, she conceived. The husband was euphoric; he started saving for a double-door fridge.

However, fate had other plans. Maybe she was not ready, maybe it wasn't meant to be. The novelty of cooking wore off. Monotony set in. The memsahib started finding more and more reasons to not enter the kitchen. Her husband let her be.

Now she's too tired to cook every day. Now she cooks only for Instagram.

Sahana Ahmed – India

Regarding Damir

Damir can't get the spices he says
so he's going back to the old country -
no marjoram, no bay-leaf, no sage.
His son Ivan tells him you can find these
in any worthwhile supermarket.
He longs for the taste of kaninchenbraten
and medimurje goose
stuffed with buckwheat.
Damir's daughter-in-law invites him over
for spaghetti bolognaise.
She can't get it through her head
that Italy is not Croatia.

Damir spends his time
packing imaginary suitcases,
selling off the microwave, the lumpy mattress,
at a yard sale,
hauling that rusty refrigerator to the dump.
He hauls out at old Atlas.
There's no Croatia
just something called Yugoslavia.
But he sees the boundary lines
even when there are none.

Damir says all his family are still there.
Ivan reminds him that almost
all the ones he remembers are dead.
How much company would
the graves of cousins provide?
But Damir can see them still,
hairy faces, rough hands,
gathered around a table
for plates of hunter's stew,
milinci and malestra,

He can hear the bellies laughing.
He can smell the garlic breath.

John Grey – Rhode Island, US

Tainted

Harriette wasn't crazy about being admitted to the psych ward of *Gut Gezunt**Hospital.

She'd be found out for the lesser Jew she was.

Fridays, when she couldn't obtain a *Shabbos goy*** to turn on or shut off the lights, she did it stealthily herself.

She not only didn't keep kosher but tore from the bone freshly fried pork, greedily devoured this *treif****, and let illicit juices escape down chin and neck — onto a blouse relegated to a corner of the bedroom. When roommates were elsewhere Harriette would throw stained clothing into the incinerator, no questions asked. Except of herself. And maybe one day a rabbi.

But did these acts constitute crazy? Why had she checked herself into a psych ward — and at Gut Gezunt?

In the first-floor apartment she shared with Raizel and Eidel, Harriette: opened windows — post-*porkfests* — to usher in breezes; sprayed Mango Zephyr air freshener through all rooms; prayed she wouldn't be found out but half hoped she would.

Male patients eighteen to early twenties devoured Gut Gezunt food. One Dietary worker told Harriette that years ago young male depressives and schizophrenics very often asked for seconds. Now each psych patient plate — even those given to females — was heaped with double-portioned proteins at lunch and dinner.

Harriette felt repulsed by colossal amounts of food, restrained herself from heaving up. She thought Gut Gezunt's system wasteful if nobly intended. Not once did she see a female patient on this ward eat more than one serving of anything — *and Harriette kept watch.*

She had decided to call shelters, inform them of extra food. Patients told her not to. Nurses, cleaning staff, too. Or had she imagined the head nurse discussing Harriette with the shower scrubber?

Had Harriette divulged to anyone on psych her guest speaker status at upcoming Dietary seminar "Future of Second Servings?" Hard to tell. Patients and staff turned Harriette's way when she entered a room. Antidepressants, however, could alter perceptions, especially those newly introduced to one's regimen.

Staff had stopped raiding her room. They conducted raids on patients who, prior to admittance to Gut Gezunt, had tried or made detailed plans to kill themselves. Early evenings, with patients less likely to be in their rooms, staff would toss dresser drawers, ferret through medicine cabinets, hunt under beds. For mirrors. Scissors. Shoelaces. Razor blades.

Harriette had fantasized cutting herself, pictured beauteous carmine streaming down her forearm. Once — just once — she imagined slowly losing her life by bingeing and purging.

At Gut Gezunt she had told this to a doctor. Harriette's breath became shallow. She placed her right hand over her mouth, remembered she'd also confessed to Raizel!

For maybe a millisecond, Harriette stopped breathing. Had she told Raizel or Eidel about the pork?

Suddenly they were there: Raizel and Eidel, as if borne to their roommate by the power of her thoughts! Young women whose long skirts swirled about their strong lower limbs. They strode to her, and they were smiling.

Her Gut Gezunt psychiatrist was somehow at her side. There were no more searches of her room because Harriette "was no longer a danger to herself." She would be signed out in two days to her roommates.

She had one question for them.

Eidel's gray-blue eyes laughed along with the rest of her. Her mouth opened wide. She touched the arm of Raizel, also clearly enjoying herself.

Eidel, between fits of laughter, said, "Harriette, *in your dreams!* There's no way you ever did that! And air fresheners? Please. We would have sniffed out pig ten blocks away. Nothing masks the odor of treif!"
The three rode home in a taxi. As soon as her roommates left, Harriette thought she'd search the back of the freezer for repackaged, relabeled meat.

Iris N Schwartz – New York, US

*Gut gezunt: Yiddish for "good health."
**Shabbos goy: a gentile who performs work on the Sabbath that a Jew can't do.
***Treif: nonkosher food, that is, food not in accord with Jewish dietary laws.

One Half Eggshell of Water

The kitchen was her kingdom
bright and warmed by the relentless sun
that poured through the glass skylight
faded the Norman Rockwell calendar from the mortuary
hanging on the wall
crinkled the appointment cards
and bleached the Congoleum floor

There she reigned supreme
on the white O'Keefe and Merritt
only one smallish oven and broiler
a pilot that went out regularly
and the clock that always read 12:30.

Those meals bound our family
the schnitzel, liver and onions,
hamburger on Wednesday nights
eaten in front of the TV to watch Superman
the tuna casserole on Thursdays
with chocolate pudding for dessert,
a thick skim on top

No different than most families
we had our share of
elephants in the living room
hulking and looming
but she stepped around them

Be polite and say thank you
her cardinal rules
drummed into us girls
though she had little patience
and we had zero interest in her kitchen
as first-generation over-achievers
driven to excel in school

Yet we do things just like her
and gleaned more from her innate sense
of dignity and propriety
than any recipes and cooking techniques
she could have shown us

Her table set and decorated just so
with linen tablecloth and napkins,
plastic flowers stuck in the silver holders
and we mastered how to perfectly garnish
the stuffed eggs with pimento and paprika
and put out the gefilte fish on crisp romaine
and don't forget the parsley

Gathered around the blonde wood dining room table
shining Sabbath candles lit
challah covered and sweet wine poured
we were infused with the rich traditions
which gave us our bearings

Passover Seders and Thanksgiving
abundant and delicious
even simple dinners served to my father
on the Formica table in the kitchen
were never thrown together
no fast food or take out
no shortcuts from a box

How was it that everything tasted better
her thick fingers working and stirring
even Good Seasons dressing mixed in the glass cruet
was different at her house my children insisted
and they were right

The comfort in knowing exactly
what would be in the green porcelain lazy Susan

for the Yom Kippur Break the Fast
the egg salad with mayo and French's mustard
the tuna with her secret
of finely chopped peppers, onions and celery
and don't forget the parsley

My cousins came from their eastern colleges
to spend holidays
to be stuffed and coddled
and to receive the common-sense wisdom
that came dished out with all her meals

Anyone who entered her door
would be enveloped in her warmth and hospitality
and you could not leave
without having a "little" something
and if she only had hot dogs in the Frig
to make for you that day
they tasted better than any you had before

A baker since childhood
before she fled Hitler's Germany
her apple cake with a soft cookie dough crust masterful
divine cherry tarts and applesauce cakes
the *Zwetschen Kuchen, Streusel Kuchen and Nuss Kuchen*
and she prepared "Ike's" chocolate birthday cake
like any proud American

And you might have been called upon
to drive over a chiffon cake to "auntie" Sadie
or deliver a honey cake for a *shivah*
or take matzoh ball soup to our Catholic neighbors
or shuttle her *hamentashen* all over on Purim

And if you were lucky to score
a tin of her chocolate chip cookies
hard in just the right way

don't even try to stop at just one
hands down the best of anything she made

And in the end when her body gave up
she could barely stand or walk
and shuffled on her walker
her hands shook
and she forgot how to make coffee
and simple meals were carried
to her on a TV tray by her helper

We dutifully brought over
filled Tupperware containers
and she was grateful for whatever we made
even preparing a scrambled egg
that was just her way

And when she passed
we gathered the precious tattered recipes
in bits and pieces, half in German
written in her backhanded scrawl
and when they called for
half an eggshell of water
we broke down and wept

For we knew we could never make her recipes
even if we could measure
a half eggshell of water
for they stood for everything she was
and they would never be the same.

Joanne Jagoda – California, US

*Zwetschen Kuchen- Plum cake- Italian plums on yeast dough
*Streusel Kuchen-Streusel Cake-butter and sugar streusel on yeast dough

*Nuss Kuchen-nut cake made of ground walnuts usually served on Passover with a chocolate glaze
*Hamenstashen-Triangular shaped cookies filled with prunes or poppy seeds traditionally made on Purim to represent Hamen's (the villain of the story) hat
*Ike's birthday cake-a chocolate cake recipe that was in the newspaper to celebrate President Eisenhower's birthday

Making Mayonnaise

It speaks to me. In paces, it softens
from shrill dissonance to fluid contralto,

keyed minor by mustard and shallot.

Everything before that is the chatter
of the oil stream spattering the scythes

of the blender, the concert of egg

and lemon drumming down to the first
fragrant breaths of a solid against

the curve of the glass. Light given body.

Who first forced yolks into olive press
or tightened vinegar with aspic?

Tarragon, spinach, or "merely parsley"

to make it proper, to mask flounder or veal,
egg mixed back into egg, cabbage, apple.

Broken yet remedied with spoons of itself.

My father talks of after-school sandwiches
with nothing but a warm swipe from the jar.

And what knock-off dressing did Grandma

whip into the Jell-O salads we picked at,
holidays held together with lecithin,

modified cornstarch? I cannot account

for my fondness of it with spring's first basil,
lending the palest green of lost memories.

Loverless, humming myself from sorrow

in my kitchen, only a bowl of cold shrimp
to bide my time this cool afternoon

just as Charles, Duke of Mayenne, may have

lingered over a dish of poached chicken
before the Huguenots forced his withdrawal.

Terry Alan Kirts – Indiana, US

Seasoning

All the small
Bottles line up to
Cascade into
Delights for
Embellishing the
Flavors. Cinnamon may be a
Good choice. Rosemary is
Handy.
If we look closely enough
Just inside the cupboard, we
Know we will find something to please us.
Looking, choosing, tasting, trying to
Make our selection seamless.
No one dominates another.
Oregano, parsley, thyme and
Pepper all
Quest together to make a
Riveting concoction –
Something spicy, something
Tantalizing. But our
Understanding of the recipe
Varies. I think of something sweet, you
Wonder about the
Xeroxed copy, now yellowed, while you
Yearn for something bitter with
Zero calories.

Deborah Purdy – Pennsylvania, US

Snake Soup

The year is rounding toward my gramma's tenth death anniversary. The date hides like a rotten seed in the reaching arc of seasons. Buried amid weeks peppered with birthdays, national holidays, and widespread religious observances, the occasion slides by unnoticed save for a faintly nauseous, poisoned feeling. Even the exact date is lost to layers of time built atop one another. The eighth? The twelfth? The details run together and marble in a dry, crusty conglomeration of stale grief and unspoken resentments. The only certain hallmark is my dad's darkened face and increased weepy references to families long since devoured by the years.

My gramma was a religious fanatic. Hellfire and brimstone were the foundations of her belief. Little boys were good American soldiers, and the only man girls needed before marriage was their Lord and Savior, Jesus Christ. In old age, her traditional Catholic values gave way to right wing televangelists and Faith Radio. I didn't know it then, at five years old. Outside of endless devotionals as birthday presents, I was not acquainted with the conservative side of her nature. To me, she was just my loving gramma, my best friend.

With the wisdom of a decade, I see now her affection for me seems less expected enjoyment of her son's only child, but more selfless adoration of angelic proportions. The hours she heaped upon me, the rules she designed for me certainly speak to her love. But more so do the rules she broke for me. There were countless standards of her religious and moral code that she tossed out and left to spoil for my happiness. And because of this, of all the days we spent playing and enjoying each other's company, the days of snake soup mean the most.

When I was a child, I owned a stuffed snake. His plush origins were unknown, his presentation dingy, his name simply "Snaky." Snaky had no special distinction, no particular place in my heart. To my gramma, he represented the devil, the great Temptation in Eden, the fall of man, but there was no way for me to know this. I did know, however, that he liked soup.

I have no idea when this idea came into my childish conscience, nor how I persuaded my gramma to indulge my whims. But I remember the green plastic bowl she set on the counter, and how she lifted me up to perch beside it. I remember the creak of the cabinet as the doors swung wide to reveal the vast horde of my dad's cooking spices, rows and rows of little glass bottles, clustered together and filled with shades of powder completing the spectrum of brown to red to dusky green. I remember the smell. It shifted from moment to moment and wafted from the darkest corners of the cabinet.

Snaky himself sat on the counter, watching over us with his glass eyes and faded velvet tongue. Under his gaze, my gramma put aside her notion that elders make the rules and allowed me to instruct her in the making of snake soup. She helped me to fill the bowl with tap water. She unscrewed the lids of jars I handed her. And she watched as I sprinkled dozens of spices into the bowl. Cumin, curry, peppercorns, and bay leaves. Nutmeg and cinnamon, coriander and oregano, paprika and poppies and tarragon. She looked over as I mutilated the flavors of twenty different cuisines. She fretted about the money I wasted, but she still handed me the marjoram from the top shelf. She complained about the mess I made, but stirred the mixture while I dashed in cardamom. She swallowed her fear of the stuffed yellow snake on the counter, slashed her misgivings about my misconduct, and offered to complete the dish with cayenne. It was her steady hand that poured in droplets of vanilla extract.

I don't know what happened to the snake soup after that. I suppose we poured it down the sink and washed away the evidence. The memory begins to blur after those moments of our cooperation. Perhaps I dreamed the whole occurrence. The mind has ways of manufacturing memories to replace the unkind void of blankness. I can never know the actuality of snake soup, if my gramma overrode her distaste of the reptile to please her granddaughter, or if my mind chose to fold sweetness into bitter reality. Now, as the anniversary drips closer like inevitable molasses, I do not care. I choose to believe: in my gramma, in myself, and in snake soup.

Marlee Head – Florida, US

Mulberries

Not one of all these berries on the ground
will sire a tree; though volunteers abound,

the lady mowing grass will never let
another tree like this extend its jet

and blackened fruit to grow; she's sure of that.
The yield is firm but now the fruit is not

as sweet as in the past when pancakes ruled.
Now berries of a different type will cool

into the batter while the batter shrinks.
I sift the colors: white and reddish pink

that switch to purple in the sun. The girls
once wore thin string to hang beneath their curls.

It held a plastic tub. They plinked their finds
from branches sweeping slowly toward the ground.

Now other pastimes fill their days with heat.
And berries strew the ground with violet streaks.

Tom Daley – Massachusetts, US

Suppertime

Standing in the kitchenette, pouring the can of Van Camp pinto beans into a saucepan, I picture the big stainless steel kettle Mom used for soups, boiling canning jars, sterilizing baby bottles, and now, as I fix my meal, I'm reminded she also used it to soak beans.

Mom had a bean formula:

1 lb. of dried beans = 2 cups
2 cups triple when cooked = 6 cups
6 cups = 8 servings

With six kids she'd usually start out with three or four pounds of dried beans.
"Nothing says you can't have leftovers."

Many mornings I'd see that kettle on the kitchen counter by the sink with floating milky husks and skins of submerged beans, soaking since before I got up. She made sure they stayed covered by an inch or so of water, never drained and rinsed like the rarely used red and white Better Homes cookbook advised.
"Why pour God's vitamins and minerals down the drain?"

She'd stir her beans occasionally, add more water and skim off the floaters until early afternoon. *"Time to start supper,"* putting the kettle on the stove while my sisters set the table.

As I shake dried onion flakes to hydrate in my warming beans, I remember the tears stung from my eyes as Mom chopped onions fresh from the garden into her pot, green parts and all. She'd rub Morton salt on her hands, *"Gets the smell off my fingers."*

While biting off the cellophane and cutting chunks of smoked beef jerky into my beans for flavor, I remember when growing up, meat wasn't always there at our house. Saved bacon grease in a Crisco can or chicken broth made do when we didn't have that ham hock or soup bone she'd sometimes get from the butcher, no matter if it were beef or pork.

My microwave pack of Sara Lee muffins is a poor replacement for the hot steaming aroma of browned yellow bricks from Mom's black tin fresh out of the oven. My sister still makes cornbread that same way and tried to tell me how.
She even wrote it down:

1 cup sifted flour
1 cup of combined yellow and white cornmeal
4 teaspoons baking powder
1 teaspoon baking soda
½ teaspoon salt
1 cup buttermilk
2 eggs
½ cup of yesterday's bacon grease
¼ cup sugar
1 tablespoon sour cream
1 tablespoon apple cider vinegar

Put flour, sugar, baking powder, salt, baking soda, cornmeal in a bowl.
Add eggs, buttermilk, sour cream, vinegar and bacon grease.
Use rotary hand mixer (never an electric mixer or blender) mix until it just gets smooth, not too much.
Pour into a buttered 9x9x2 inch pan
Bake at 425 degrees for 25 minutes

Carrying my meal, still in the saucepan to the foldout metal tray table by the couch, I think back to our family supper table…

We wait for Mom to take off her apron and sit at her end of the table. Dad sits on the other end, three boys on one side, three girls on the other. She ladles out eight bowls of steaming hot beans beside a 3x3 inch cornbread cake and a cold glass of fresh cow's milk.

Together we say grace while smiling at the feast in front of us. With a chorus of *"Father, Son, Holy Ghost"* and a nod from Dad, we all dig in.

"Amen," I whisper to my quiet room and turn up the sound on the apartment TV.

Carl "Papa" Palmer – Washington, US

Cooking for the Cat

could never cook for myself,
(I) (it) did not seem worth the trouble
to chop up onions and garlic,

to look for seasonings on the pantry shelf,
to set out a place mat, plate, knife and fork,
to serve myself

when there are so many drive-through windows,
quick anonymous transactions:
here, ma'am, is your change--

so, I tried to throw out my wok,
but it sat there on top of the trash bin
like a rejected pet,

its surface scarred and dented
seasoned with old oils,
the handles that always were too hot to touch

poking out from yesterday's news,
so, I thought I would give it one more go
and I chopped up onions and garlic,

threw in shrimp, noodles,
ginger, celery, a wilted pepper,
and a burst of festive scent filled the house,

and I said *ohhh, how good* to the cat,
slipped her slivers of shrimp while we watched the news--
then she played with a noodle

as I wiped dry the battered wok,
put it back into the cabinet.
we were worth it.

Janet McCann – Texas, US

A Student Supper

Clutching coins rescued
from dunes of denim,
Zack and I strode into Store 24 and
scanned the constellation of instant noodles:
a pink shrimp packet for him
and mud-colored mushroom for me
because I'd vowed
not to devour anything with a heartbeat.

Across Thayer Street and three flights up,
we crackled the slick wrappers between our fingers
before loading his electric teakettle and my hot pot
with pulsating streams of tap water.

While the Rolling Stones leaked out of the radio,
we plugged our appliances into gaping black sockets
and waited-but didn't look- for Mom
had warned that a watched pot never boils.
So we flipped pages of *Njal's Saga*
since a professor with the power to flunk
expected convincing essays in eight hours.

When the crescendo of bubbles crept across the dorm room,
we bathed the bricks of wiggly carbs
as stiff as Medusa's hair-
if she were the one turned to stone-
and for three minutes I worried needlessly
that a wire lurking unseen would spark.

Then we ripped open our square silver sachets.
Our nostrils quivered from
the briny fragrance of flavor dust
as we stirred with white plastic sporks
salvaged from a forgotten fast-food feast.

Slurping up savory heat-bursts
of broth and worms of wheat
assuaged by chilly swigs of Crystal Pepsi,
we were determined to defeat the deadline –
driven by MSG, sugar and slaphappy silliness.

Adrian Slonaker – Iowa, US

Reimagining Olives

We were broke when we first moved
in together, got by on clipping
coupons. We watched *Chopped* enough

to know how to repurpose
groceries: salvage components of last night's
dinner and reimagine them

into tomorrow's lunch.
Today I learned to tapenade
with yesterday's black olives. Next week

I'll attempt to stir-fry
the leftovers I'll take
from eating with my mother

at home.

I still call her house *home*
even though I haven't lived there
in almost three years.

My bedroom of two and a half decades
is now a guest room,
but I'm no guest.

I'll still go in, close the door behind me
when I need a break. I still lie
on the sun-faded, purple carpet

that soaked up my teenage tears
from boys who came and went. I'll finger
the spot that took a burning

from a forgotten flatiron, tear up thinking

I neglected a foundation
that always embraced me. And while I now

have you, with all my free time spent busy
budgeting and reimagining my food
to make it more interesting,

I guess I haven't quite yet reimagined home.

Shelby Lynn Lanaro – Connecticut, US

Thanksgiving

The kitchen dense with heat,
turkey, mother juggled chestnuts,

squash, stuffing, her miracle
to fill the table, to fill

her family, but not enough
we cannot eat enough for

her our thanks are not
enough, the beauty and plenty

of the table, the sweat, burnt
arm, sliced finger, the picked-clean

bones afterwards, not enough when
from every mirror her own mother asks
"Who are you fooling?"

Jonathan B Aibel – Massachusetts, US

Letting the Cat Out

Fork the length of the piping hot potato
as you might prepare hard spring soil.

Make the sign of the cross
by tilling the other way.

Squeeze both ends, being careful not to burn your fingers.
One or two butter pats, salt and pepper over that.

Soy sauce goes on the table, as accompaniment—
you'll never again eat a baked potato

any other way. Salt the cantaloupe,
serve salad with—not before

nor after dinner. Cocktails first,
and a dressing drink before that.

Count to ten while blanching
tomatoes in boiling water, as she once taught you,

standing stove-side, in her sheer black apron,
a Diane von Furstenberg under that,

third vodka in the other hand.
Learn to hold liquor like secrets

you swore never to tell.
Later, when you think of calling her

after the abortion or divorce,
let the phone rest silent on its cradle.

Or tell her he wronged you first

though it was the other way around.

Offer always to do the dishes,
eating as much as you can

from the abandoned plates of those privileged enough
to leave some food behind—then, close the bathroom door.

When she asks where all the leftovers went,
stare blankly, or lie. Some things she oughtn't know.

Don't answer the phone, text her in heaven;
it's what's left of your family.

That, and these foods, this bread,
soy sauce on a baked potato.

Julia Wendell – South Carolina, US

Twenty Ways Cooking Is a Liability to My Love Life

because to garnish takes too long and who eats the parsley anyway

because the wood of a table and chairs is foreign is finished

because putting down the phone

because jazz on the speakers, because candles

because *beurre blanc, mise-en-place, chiffonade*

because not a recipe from a Food Network star

because they have that at Panera at Chipotle on the hot bar at Whole Foods at Applebee's

because wine

because wine not with a cartoon of a kangaroo or the sleek figure of Marilyn Monroe

because no binging our shows

because weighing the flour instead of measuring with cups

because dishes

because I insist on rinsing before the dishwasher

because despite a century of feminism the kitchen is still essentially an objective space where two men can only compete or cancel each other

because *two hours to cook what we eat in fifteen?*

because I really just came over for sex

because giving instead of taking, because the true romantic loves only what will consume him

because *you expect me to eat that?*

because I meal prep, I don't cook

because Instagram posts of delicious-looking dinners make people think I am actually fulfilled

Terry Alan Kirts – Indiana, US

Breakfast Poem

Why do you wake up so late in the morning, only when rush-hour traffic has split the doves' chatter to industrial screeching, and all I can turn to is the rhythm of your heart?

I wish we could talk over scrambled eggs and hazelnut coffee, when the road is tongue-tied, and the grass out back is awash in orange under the sunrise.

Just a half-hour meal would feel like days, we'd talk about your beautiful dreams and what to do with ourselves on hot Saturday nights when comforters don't.

For once the sky wouldn't be so melancholy, like when the clouds come low and smother us, soaking up our aspirations for a pretty day in pastel fog.

When it's chilly, my pillows are cold as marble countertops. The bedside lamp radiates a mellow glow, but the fog chokes it out and I move by your siren song.

Your voice is crisp and sweet. When the birds are gone I think of how you said my surname that first time. Oh, I don't remember who I was before we met.

Samuel Swauger – Maryland, US

Cookbook

1.
She chops gefülte fish (enough for a crowd) for two hours;
bakes challah; pours out honey (thick, dark) into a bowl;
cuts apples; everything for a sweet new year.

The fall air heats damp and unrelenting.

The rabbi says, *Ask what the other needs
not as you go out the door*—the reply, detergent
or blades, at least is clean
and sharp—
      *ask what the other needs
as you come in.*

She asks, but her husband's grin cuts
into stone.

2.
Party Time

Alice B's in the refrigerator
wrapped in foil
perhaps in a brown paper bag.

Reds in the medicine cabinet;
a new valium prescription in her purse.

The wet bar:
Wild Turkey over.
Tanqueray up.

Coke mixer.

She sheds her shoes.
Her hair shreds under lacquer.

One eyelash droops.

He leaves with someone else.
She doesn't notice.
The music stops.

3.
Who was that young thing
who baked cherry pies?
Billy in the bedroom
telling all his lies
sends her for his slippers;
sends her for his meat;
then points to her zippers,
lays her at his feet.

4.
love apples
potato praise

she cooks for a living:
gulyás with 1/4 cup of paprika
18 cloves of garlic
18 lovers in the garden with rosemary
no salt
no fat
no flour
flowers

sweet peas growing on the fence
nasturtium peppery petals
dandelion tongue rough
Persephone's seven pomegranate seeds
all seasons thyme

ravenously
he eats

5.
Japanese plate:

pale pink fan of raw tuna
cluster of fine white shredded daikon
wasabi
chrysanthemum leaf

she lifts the skirt of her kimono

6.
The Meal:

dried fig seeds shiver
against her teeth;

they nibble at kernels of corn,
bits of spiced beef:

caraway, coriander, a sprinkle
of mandrake powder;

he sips wine, bites
into morsels of fruit;

they eat lotus cakes,
wet their lips with orgeat syrup;

her tongue licks dark
grapes, the juice red on her mouth;

his beard knits into
her hair;

avocado traces on her lips brown
in the air, not quite licked clean.

7.
Seasons

The poison is sour
in his soup.
Still he eats it:
strands of celery,
the thick mélange of split
pea lentil barley.

At the last mouthful
he looks up at her.
Delicious, he says;
lays his head
down on the table as if the statement
were too great an effort;
then is still.

She expected more.
A few spasms.
Maybe a howl or
doubling up.
She is disappointed
and turns
to wake from the dream.
He is lying there
in the bed
not breathing,
a grain of barley caught
between his front teeth.

She gets up
no light
no slippers
gropes to the bathroom;

his snore catches breath
behind her.

She thinks, He should floss
more carefully. She thinks, Even
in a dream to be capable of
murder. Cold air on her legs; the hair
pricks up; a long night
soon winter, longer yet.

Stephanie Pressman – California, US

Skillet

The matching towels and Tupperware came and went
but the cast-iron skillet we got as a wedding gift
all those years ago is going strong.
So many years, you think it's from your grandma.

That cast-iron skillet we got as a wedding gift
was really from my aunt. Of that I'm sure.
So many years, you think. Like graying hair,
the skillet so old it's new again. Even hip

(and really from my aunt). I'm sure
the meals we make are better now.
Cast iron so old it's new again, and hip
thanks to fancy cookbooks and Instagram.

The meals we make are better. Now
all those years and that skillet's going strong.
The fancy cookbooks and Instagram
match like towels. The Tupperware came and went.

Jackie Fox – Nebraska, US

The Afghani Chicken

The aroma of cloves, cardamom and cinnamon floated from one room to the other. The rusty flavor of roasting onions in homemade buffalo Ghee(clarified butter) swirled out from the kitchen and unfurled its blanket on the open veranda where the cracks on the walls were exposed to their skeleton. Slowly it rolled to the bedroom on the other side of the veranda where Mithilesh was reading a book on contemporary art. Sunday is the only day when he finds some time for himself. Tito was playing in the veranda. Mithilesh can see him from his armchair, striking the tiny metal balls with the bagatelle stick. This was his childhood board game which was kept safely so far by his mother and now gifted to Tito. Old games like these are now gradually vanishing from the toy shops. The various types of games they used to enjoy at their childhood are all getting replaced rapidly by the virtual game world of the computers.

The marinated chicken was poured in the ghee. Curd, cashew nut, ginger garlic paste softly got stirred with the wooden spatula on a low flame. The aroma of the cuisine levitating from the kitchen was enough to tempt even a non-foodie like Mithilesh. His wife, Keka is a great cook always coming up with delicious new dishes. Mithilesh always appreciates this quality of hers in his mind but could never pour down in audible words. He is a very quiet person and less expressive in his emotions. Keka keeps on muttering about this but the basic human nature is hard to change.

The heavenly fragrance of rose water which just got added to the Afghani chicken watered the mouth of the seven years old. Tito waddled to the kitchen with his bagatelle. But his little hands with unstable balancing skills tilted the bagatelle in midway and dropped all its little metal balls just in front of the kitchen door. The balls bounced off to different directions. Some behind the flowerpot by the kitchen door. Some under the big wooden chest filled with age old bronze utensils. Some even inside the kitchen where he could see his mother grinding a bunch of dry masalas in their old marble mortar and pestle set. Tito put down the empty bagatelle in front of the kitchen door and scratched his head. He sat down on his knees bending his head low and got busy seeking the tiny balls from their hiding place. He slipped his little hand under the huge wooden chest and moved to and fro to search them. He got one and then another, the little fingers continued hobbling around as he heard his mom talking over phone. It's Rudy uncle she was talking to. Rudy uncle is a musician. He knows how to play the piano. They went to his house several times. Where there is a big piano kept in the huge black and white sitting room. Tito saw him playing it several times. Mom was still Talking when Tito wobbled around her searching his tiny bagatelle balls. Tito got almost all of his balls and kept them back on the board again. This time he took it up carefully and slowly went back to his Papa balancing the tiny balls rolling all over the board.

"What is it Tito?" Mithilesh asked softy pulling Tito near to his lap. "I lost two balls" he answered. "I slipped the bagatelle in front of the kitchen door and all the balls rolled here and there. I got them back but two are still missing" the tiny voice said with a note of sadness in it. "Why didn't you ask Mom to find them back?" Mithilesh asked pampering Tito with a kiss. "Mom was talking to Rudy Uncle. She was inviting him for lunch today. She was saying you never appreciate any of mom's cooking, and she doesn't like to cook for you anymore. She said she loves to cook for Rudy uncle and today she cooked his favorite dish Afghani chicken. She requested him to come and said she will be eagerly waiting for him." Mithilesh couldn't say a word, he froze on his armchair as the magnificent smell of mace and nutmeg smothered his heart.

Debjani Mukherjee – India

All the Souvenirs

everything tastes better in bed
you whispered in my ear
too many times

I smashed all the souvenirs from the places
you always wanted to visit
shouting out her name

shattered pieces getting deep
into your Persian carpet
like knives into flesh

frantically trying to change a hoover bag
and everything else in my life
job flat breakfast cereal

no more take away pizza
from that Italian place
on the corner

we were always forgetting napkins
and you were licking
my fingers

Agnieszka Filipek – Ireland

Barbecued Poem

For the marinade, combine:

Three cups of granulated clouds
One quart of chopped observations
A handful of peppercorns
A pint of insight
A jigger of color
A pinch of whimsy

Add to this mixture—
as many birds as possible.

Remove any stray adverbs.
Cover and refrigerate overnight.

Heat the grill to 325:
Before placing on grill,
remove peppercorns
and unintended end rhyme.

After 20 minutes:

Flip the birds!
Baste with alliteration
and sprinkle with
words you've never used before.
Words like *pellucid* and *luculent*.

When the poem seems done:
Remove from heat.
Let rest for at least 10 minutes.
Season the birds to taste with
additional made-up attributes.

Before serving:

Chop every 4th line and at least one stanza.
Arrange on platter.
Re-arrange on platter.

Optional: Garnish with false modesty
or macerated self-praise.

Louise Hofmeister – California, US

Cornbread Without Butter

That takeout Chinese food has left me in the mood
for some down home cookin'. Can't get to sleep starin' at your
empty pillow. In the moonlight it glows.

And now it's three a.m., and I'm hungry again.
I went to the kitchen to look for some fixin's.
I found your cold skillet with no cornpone in it.

I'm like cornbread without butter,
my bed without a lover.
I can't find another
who bakes it hot like you.

Cornbread and butter,
the two need each other.
Life without a partner
has left me sad and blue.

Now I'm cornbread without butter without you.

At our wedding banquet you had quite a fit
when the caterers served crackers with the hors d'oeuvres.
You, in your wedding dress, baked cornbread for the guests.

And, on our honeymoon in the middle of June,
you slathered my body's ev'ry nook and cranny.
Now you left me alone while my love for you groans.
I'm like cornbread without butter,
my bed without a lover.
I can't find another
who bakes it hot like you.

Cornbread and butter,
the two need each other.

Life without a partner
has left me sad and blue.

Now I'm cornbread without butter without you.

The way to a man's heart is through his tummy
when a woman cooks for him somethin' yummy.

The way to a woman's heart is through her mind
when a man is satisfied, faithful, and kind.

At the Piggly Wiggly, don't know what got in me,
I searched along the aisles, hopin' to find your smile.
I'd first noticed you here when your voice caught my ear.

You had squealed at the deal on corn to grind to meal.
Now you've got up and gone. Woman, I did you wrong.
I sure made a mistake in your sister's Easy-Bake.

I'm like cornbread without butter,
my bed without a lover.
I can't find another
who bakes it hot like you.

Cornbread and butter,
the two need each other.
Life without a partner
has left me sad and blue.

Now I'm cornbread without butter without you.
Now I'm cornbread without butter without you.

André Wilson – California, US

Cornbread Without Butter

words and music by André Le Mont Wilson

c 2019 André Le Mont Wilson

Author Biographies

Sahana Ahmed is a fiction writer from Bengaluru, India. Her work has appeared in Flash: The International Short-Short Story Magazine and The Hindu BusinessLine among others. She is the author of *Combat Skirts* (Juggernaut Books, 2018; Quignog, 2018). Visit her online at www.sahanaahmed.com.

Jonathan B. Aibel is a poet who spends his days wrestling software to the ground as an engineer specializing in quality and testing. His poems have been published, or will soon appear, in *Rogue Agent, Main Street Rag, Constellations, Nixes Mate, Lily Poetry Review,* and elsewhere. He has studied with Lucie Brock-Broido, David Ferry and Barbara Helfgott Hyett. Jonathan lives in Concord, MA with his family.

Brian Alvarado is a sonnet, bel canto opera, and craft beer enthusiast, born and raised in the Bronx. He has been featured in print in: Susquehanna University's RiverCraft, VCFA's Trailhead, The Bay View Literary Magazine, and DenimSkin Review, and online in: Contraposition, The Insomniac Propagandist, and Squawk Back, among others. He holds a degree in Creative Writing from Susquehanna University.

Elvis Alves is the author of Bitter Melon (2013), Ota Benga (2017), and I Am No Battlefield But A Forest Of Tress Growing (2018), winner of the Jacopone da Todi poetry book prize. Elvis lives in New York City with his family.

Jacqueline Anderson currently lives in the city Rockport on the Texas coast. She is a member of the Aransas County Poetry Society. Her other work has been published by Gabriel's Horn Press in the 2019 Annual Anthology, *Startled by Joy.*

Glen Armstrong holds an MFA in English from the University of Massachusetts, Amherst and teaches writing at Oakland University in Rochester, Michigan. He edits a poetry journal called *Cruel Garters* and has two new chapbooks: *Simpler Times* and *Staring Down Miracles.* His work has appeared in *Poetry Northwest, Conduit,* and *Cream City Review.*

KB Baltz was born in a Cosmic Hamlet by the Sea a month early and backwards. She has been doing things sideways ever since. As the offspring of a hippie and a commercial fisherman she is all about peace, love, and fish and is a bit confused about the whole thing. When she isn't writing KB can be found hiking in the great Alaskan outdoors.

Amy Barnes has words at a variety of sites including McSweeney's, We Were So Small, Parabola, FlashBack Fiction, Detritus, and The New Southern Fugitives.

Elizabeth Beck is the author of three books of poetry. In 2011, I founded the Teen Howl Poetry Series that serves the youth of central Kentucky while also leading an award-winning middle school poetry group called Leestown OUTLOUD.

John T. Biggs describes himself as a regional writer whose region is somewhere west of the Twilight Zone. Sixty of John's short stories have been published in magazines and anthologies that vary from literary to young adult speculative fiction. He has won regional and national awards including Grand Prize in the Writers Digest 80th annual competition. John has published four novels: *Owl Dreams*, *Popsicle Styx*, *Cherokee*, and *Shiners*, and a series of post-apocalyptic novellas, *Clementine a song for the end of the world*.

Jane Blanchard lives and writes in Georgia. Her poetry has been published around the world as well as posted online. Her collections----the shorter *Unloosed* and the longer *Tides & Currents*—are available from Kelsay Books.

Jeff Burt lives in Santa Cruz County, California. He has work in Rabid Oak, Pendora, The Monarch Review, and Cold Mountain Review.

Caroliena Cabada is an MFA candidate at Iowa State University and holds a BA in Chemistry from New York University. Her writing has been published in The Minetta Review.

Fern G. Z. Carr is a former lawyer, teacher and past President of both the Society for the Prevention of Cruelty to Animals and Project Literacy Central Okanagan Society. A Full Member of and former Poet-in-Residence for the League of Canadian Poets, this Pushcart Prize nominee composes and translates poetry in six languages. Carr has been published extensively worldwide from Finland to Mauritius and has had her work recognized by the Parliamentary Poet Laureate. Her poetry collection, *Shards of Crystal* (Silver Bow Publishing, 2018), is available on Amazon. Carr is thrilled to have one of her poems currently orbiting the planet Mars aboard NASA'S MAVEN spacecraft.

Ann Cefola is the author of *Free Ferry* (Upper Hand Press, 2017), and *Face Painting in the Dark* (Dos Madres Press, 2014); translator of

Alparegho, like nothing else (The Operating System, 2019), *The Hero* (Chax Press, 2018), and *Hence this cradle* (Seismicity Editions, 2007); and recipient of the Robert Penn Warren Award judged by John Ashbery.

Kersten Christianson is a raven-watching, moon-gazing Alaskan. She holds an MFA in Creative Writing (University of Alaska Anchorage), has authored two books of poetry – *What Caught Raven's Eye* (Petroglyph Press, 2018) and *Something Yet to Be Named* (Aldrich Press, 2017) – and is the poetry editor of *Alaska Women Speak*.

Christine Collier is the author of many cozy mysteries and published in anthology books by Guideposts, Adams Media, HCI Ultimate Books, Smoking Pen Press, Wagonbridge Publishing, Silver Boomer Books, Silver Birch Press, Write Integrity, and more.

Ronald K. Craig, PhD, is a retired psychology professor. His haiku have been published in several journals, anthologies and blogs. He and his wife live in the Cincinnati, Ohio area. He has one adult daughter. As an Ohio Certified Volunteer Naturalist he practices stewardship at the Cincinnati Nature Center.

Linda M. Crate's poetry, short stories, articles, and reviews have been published in a myriad of magazines both online and in print. She has six published chapbooks including *My Wings Were Made to Fly* (Flutter Press, September 2017), *splintered with terror* (Scars Publications, January 2018), *more than bone music* (Clare Songbirds Publishing House, March 2019), and one micro-chapbook *Heaven Instead* (Origami Poems Project, May 2018). She is also the author of the novel *Phoenix Tears* (Czykmate Books, June 2018).

Lauren Cutrone is a marketing coordinator for a small children's book company based in New Jersey. She is also a contributing writer for *The Mighty* where she writes about mental health. Recently, Lauren has been featured as a poet for Nancy Smith's *Women Speak* project and has been included as a contributing writer for the book *Alcott's Imaginary Heroes: The Little Women Legacy*. When she isn't writing, she's listening to opera, petting dogs, and collecting garden gnomes. Lauren can be reached at lecutrone@gmail.com.

Tom Daley's poetry has appeared in *Harvard Review, Massachusetts Review, 32 Poems, Fence, Denver Quarterly, Crazyhorse, Barrow Street, Prairie Schooner*, among others. He is the recipient of the Fanny Fay Wood Prize from the Academy of American Poets, he is the author of two plays, *Every Broom and Bridget—Emily Dickinson and Her Irish*

Servants and *In His Ecstasy—The Passion of Gerard Manley Hopkins*, and a book of poetry, *House You Cannot Reach—Poems in the Voice of My Mother and Other Poems* (Future Cycle Press, 2015). He leads writing workshops in the Boston area and online for poets and writers working in creative prose.

Neil Davidson is a fiction writer with a B.A. in English from the University of Oregon and an M.A. in English from the University of California, Davis. A former cook, his work frequently focuses on the service industry, labor practices, and the hospitality traditions that surround food. His work has previously appeared in "Unbound: Literary Arts Magazine" as well as several anthologies, including "FLASH! Fiction Anthology" and "Mother's Revenge."

Merridawn Duckler is a writer from Portland, Oregon, author of INTERSTATE, dancing girl press and IDIOM, winner of the Washburn Prize. Recent work in Ninth Letter, Pithead Chapel, Queen Mob's Tea House, Emry's. Fellowships/awards include Yaddo, Southampton Poetry Conference, Poets on the Coast, Sundress Academy, best of the net nomination. She's an editor at Narrative and at the philosophy journal Evental Aesthetics.

Catherine Edmunds is a writer, artist and folk/rock fiddle player. Her published works include two poetry collections, four novels and a Holocaust memoir. She has been nominated three times for a Pushcart Prize, shortlisted in the Bridport four times, and has works in journals including Aesthetica, Crannóg and Ambit.

Les Epstein is a poet, playwright and opera librettist. His work has appeared in journals in the United States, Philippines, India and the U.K. Recent credits include *Eyedrum Periodically, Interstice, Mojave River Review, Fourth & Sycamore, and Saudade. Cyberwit* recently released a collection of his short plays and libretti (*Seven*). His poems were recently featured in the podcast, "Sunflower Sutras," broadcast out of Washburn University. He teaches in Roanoke, VA.

Sarah Evans has had many short stories published in anthologies, literary journals and online. Her stories have been shortlisted by the Commonwealth Short Story Prize and been awarded prizes by, amongst others: Words and Women, Stratford Literary Festival and the Bridport Prize. Her work is also included in several Unthology volumes, Best New Writing and Shooter Magazine.

Agnieszka Filipek lives in Galway, Ireland. She writes in both, her native tongue Polish and in English, and also translates in these languages. Her work has been published internationally in countries, such as Poland, Ireland, India, China, England, Wales, Germany, Bangladesh, Canada and the United States. Her poems have appeared in *Marble Poetry Magazine, Pale Fire – New Writing on the Moon Anthology, Crannóg, The Stony Thursday Book, Chrysanthemum* and other publications. For more visit www.agnieszkafilipek.com

Albuquerque, New Mexico, writer Mark Fleisher has published three books of poetry -- with a little prose and some photographs thrown in -- and collaborated on a fourth. His work has also appeared in numerous anthologies, both in print and on line. A native of Brooklyn, New York, Fleisher earned a bachelor's degree in journalism from Ohio University. His four years in the U.S. Air Force included a year in Vietnam as a combat news reporter. He received a Bronze Star for meritorious service.

Jackie Fox's poetry has appeared in a range of journals and anthologies including Rattle, The Fem, Tar River Poetry, The Bellevue Literary Review, The Untidy Season: An Anthology of Nebraska Women Poets, BARED: Contemporary Poetry and Art on Bras and Breasts, and Ted Kooser's American Life in Poetry column.

Jack M. Freedman is a poet and spoken word artist from Staten Island, NY. Publications featuring his work span the globe. Countries include USA, Canada, UK, France, The Netherlands, Ukraine, India, Nigeria, Singapore, and Thailand. He is the author of the upcoming chapbook, ...and the willow smiled (Cyberwit.net, 2019).

Cynthia Gallaher, a Chicago-based poet and playwright, is author of four poetry collections, including *Epicurean Ecstasy: More Poems About Food, Drink, Herbs and Spices* (The Poetry Box, Portland, 2019), and three chapbooks, including *Drenched* (Main Street Rag, Charlotte, N.C., 2018), poems about liquids. The Chicago Public Library lists her among its "Top Ten Requested Chicago Poets."

James Gering's poetry and fiction have garnered awards and have appeared in a number of journals including Rattle, the Rockvale Review and the San Pedro River Review. He holds a Masters in Creative Writing and received the Australian Society of Authors Emerging Poet of the Year award, 2018. More information about him and his publications can be found at jamesgering.com. When not writing, he teaches English at the University of Sydney in Australia. He also revels in nature – climbing, canyoning and running trails in the pristine Blue Mountains near Sydney.

Sandy Green writes from her home in Virginia where her work has appeared in such places as Bitter Oleander, Northern Virginia Review, Existere, Poetry South, and Qwerty, as well as in her chapbook, Pacing the Moon (Flutter Press, 2009). She has recently completed a second chapbook manuscript, Lot for Sale. No Pigs, forthcoming from BatCat Press in June 2019.

John Grey is an Australian poet, US resident. Recently published in Midwest Quarterly, Poetry East and North Dakota Quarterly with work upcoming in South Florida Poetry Journal, Hawaii Review and the Dunes Review.

Marlee Head's work has appeared in the online magazines Verse of Silence and Potato Soup Journal. She has also been published in the recent Pearson textbook Reading Literature and Writing Argument. She attended the 2019 Iceland Writers Retreat in April.

Cambria Hines is a freelance poet and writer from central Iowa. She lives in a happy home with her boyfriend and their children, who are two fuzzy kitties. Cambria has traveled the country and draws from both her positive and negative experiences to write her short fictional stories and poems. When she is not fighting writers block, you can find her binge watching Netflix and putting shirts on her cats.

Louise Hofmeister-After a long career that included lots of technical writing, I decided to pursue some more creative expression upon my recent retirement. I found my post-career haven in Petaluma, California, where I am the happy next door neighbor of a chorus of roosters, a covey of quail and one amazing caterwauling donkey. In the past two years, I had four poems included in the regional *Redwood Writers Anthology* and three picked up for publication by *Truth Serum* and *Pure Slush*.

Juleigh Howard-Hobson has appeared in many places on and off line, including *The Quality Journal of Food and Car Poems, The Ghost City Review, Coffin Bell Journal, The Literary Hatchet, The Shooter, Non Binary Review,* "The Literary Whip" (the podcast of the Nonbinary Review), The Nancy Drew Anthology (Silver Birch), Mandragora (Scarlett Imprint), The 2018 Rhysling Anthology (The Science Fiction Poetry Association) and many others. She edited an Arêtes Vakreste Boker award winning Norwegian anthology: Undertow. She has served as assistant poetry editor at *Able Muse*. She is a *Story South*/Million Writers Award "Notable Story" writer, a Predators and Editor's top ten finisher. She has been nominated for the Best of the Net, the Pushcart Prize, and the Rhysling. She has five poetry books published. Her most recent collection is Our Otherworld (The Red Salon Press, 2018)

Justin Hunter has nine published novels, award winning screenplays, and over thirty short stories published in anthologies. He lives with his wife and four adopted children in Missouri. Follow him on Twitter - @JustinJAHunter

Natalie E. Illum is a poet, disability activist and singer living in Washington DC. She is a recipient of 2 Poetry Fellowships from the DC Arts Commission, a former Jenny McKean Moore Fellow and an editor for The Deaf Poets Society Literary Journal. She was a founded board member of mothertongue DC, an LGBTQA open mic that lasted 15 years. She competed on the National Poetry Slam circuit and was the 2013 Beltway Grand Slam Champion. She is currently a Pushcart Prize, Best New Poet, and Best of the Net nominee. Natalie has an MFA in Creative Writing from American University. You can find her on Instagram and Twitter as @poetryrox, and as one half of All Her Muses. Natalie loves whiskey and giraffes.

After retiring in 2009, one inspiring writing workshop in the Amherst method launched Joanne Jagoda of Oakland, California on an unexpected writing trajectory. Her stories, poetry and creative nonfiction appear on-line and in numerous print anthologies and include a Pushcart nomination and first place awards in several contests. Forthcoming 2019 publications which will include her poetry are Dreamers Creative Writing and Passager Journal. Creative writing has helped her navigate through her breast cancer journey and the serious illness of her husband. Joanne continues taking Bay Area writing workshops, enjoys Zumba, traveling and spoiling her seven grandchildren who call her "Savta.".

Sarah Jane Justice is an accomplished writer over many genres. After completing several professional recordings as a singer-songwriter, and performing an original one woman show in the 2016 Adelaide Fringe Festival, she has achieved most of her success in spoken word poetry, winning numerous awards and performing at the National Finals of the Australian Poetry Slam in 2018.

Diane Kendig's recent collections include her poetry *Prison Terms* and an anthology she co-edited, *In the Company of Russell Atkins*. A recipient of Ohio Arts Council Fellowships in Poetry and other awards, she has published poetry and prose in journals such as *J Journal, Under the Sun*, and *Blueline*. She curates the Cuyahoga County website, "Read + Write: 30 Days of Poetry," now in its sixth year. Her website is dianekendig.com

Terry Kirts is the author of *To the Refrigerator Gods*, which was chosen for the Editor's Choice series in poetry by Seven Kitchen's Press in 2010. He is a senior lecturer in creative writing at Indiana University-Purdue University in Indianapolis. His poetry and creative nonfiction have appeared or are forthcoming in such journals as *Third Coast, Gastronomica, Alimentum, Sycamore Review, Green Mountains Review,* and *Another Chicago Magazine*, as well as the anthologies *Food Poems* and *Home Again: Essays and Memoirs from Indiana*. His culinary articles and restaurant reviews have appeared in *WHERE Indianapolis, Indianapolis Woman, Nuvo,* and *Indianapolis Dine*, and he is currently a dining critic for *Indianapolis Monthly*.

Shelby Lynn Lanaro is a poet by passion and teacher by trade. She received her MFA in 2017 from Southern Connecticut State University, where she now teaches Freshman English. A New England native, Shelby has an acute attention to nature and capturing its splendor through words and photography. Shelby's poems and photographs have appeared or are forthcoming in *The Feminist Wire, Dying Dahlia Review, Stormy Island Publishing, Poetry Breakfast, Young Ravens Literary Review, Voice of Eve,* and *The Wild Word*.

Joan Leotta is a writer and story performer who takes page and stage with poems, articles, essays, and stories that often feature food. Her work has been published in Postcard Poems and Prose, The Lake, Sasee, When Women Write, Social Justice Poetry, and many other fine print and online journals and magazines. When she is not writing or in the kitchen you can find walking the beach hunting for shells.

Fabiyas M V is a writer from Orumanayur village in Kerala, India. He is the author of Kanoli Kaleidoscope (PunksWritePoemsPress,US), Eternal Fragments (erbacce press,UK), and Moonlight And Solitude (Raspberry Books, India). His fiction and poetry have appeared in several anthologies, magazines and journals. He has won many international accolades including Merseyside at War Poetry Award from Liverpool University and Poetry Soup International Award. He was the finalist for Global Poetry Prize 2015 by the United Poets Laureate

International (UPLI) in Vienna. His poems have been broadcast on All India Radio. Poetry Nook, US, has nominated him for the 2019 Pushcart Prize. He has been working as a teacher in English at Gov. Higher Secondary School, Maranchery in Kerala.

Michal Mahgerefteh is an award-winning poet and artist from Norfolk, Virginia. She is the author of four poetry collection, currently working on her fifth and six collections. Michal is the managing editor of Mizmor Anthology and Anna Davidson Rosenberg Poetry Award. Her writings were recently published by Edify Fiction Magazine, Ekphrastic Review, Eve Anthology, and The Jewish Literary Magazine.

DS Maolalai has been nominated for Best of the Web and twice for the Pushcart Prize. His poetry has been released in two collections, "Love is Breaking Plates in the Garden" (Encircle Press, 2016) and "Sad Havoc Among the Birds" (Turas Press, 2019).

Johnny Masiulewicz is author of the poetry collection Professional Cemetery (Puddin'head Press) and creator of the *Happy Tapir* zine series. His work has appeared in a variety of literary journals, anthologies and sites including *Curbside Review, The Main Street Rag, Third Wednesday, Nerve Cowboy* and *The Alembic*. A native Chicagoan, he now lives and works in Jacksonville, Florida

Janet McCann is a crone poet who taught teaching creative writing at Texas A&M from 1969 until 2015. Journals publishing her work include KANSAS QUARTERLY, PARNASSUS, NIMROD, SOU'WESTER, CHRISTIAN CENTURY, CHRISTIANITY AND LITERATURE, NEW YORK QUARTERLY, TENDRIL, POETRY AUSTRALIA, among many others. She has won five chapbook contests, sponsored by Pudding Publications, Chimera Connections, Franciscan University Press, Plan B Press, and Sacramento Poetry Center. A 1989 NEA Creative Writing Fellowship winner, she is co-ordinator of creative writing here. Her most recent book-length collection: THE CRONE AT THE CASINO, Lamar UP, 2015.

Matt McGee writes short fiction in the Los Angeles area. In 2019, his stories 'Here's a Story' appeared in LA's Poetic Diversity and 'The Rebirthing Shed' will appear in Zimbell House's "1929" anthology. His first novel 'Wildwood Mountain' was released June 19th by Melange Books. When not typing he drives around in a vintage Mazda and plays goalie in local hockey leagues.

Bob McNeil is the author of *Verses of Realness*. Hal Sirowitz, Queens Poet Laureate, described the book as "A fantastic trip through the mind of a poet who doesn't flinch at the truth." Bob was published in *The Shout It Out Anthology*, *Brine Rights: Stanzas and Clauses for the Causes (Volume 1)*, *San Francisco Peace and Hope*, and *The Self-Portrait Poetry Collection*, etc. Furthermore, Bob's work as a professional illustrator, spoken word artist, and writer is dedicated to one cause—justice.

Joan McNerney's poetry has been included in numerous literary magazines such as Seven Circle Press, Dinner with the Muse, Moonlight Dreamers of Yellow Haze, Blueline, and Halcyon Days. Four Bright Hills Press Anthologies, several Poppy Road Review Journals, and numerous Kind of A Hurricane Press Publications have accepted her work. Her latest title is Having Lunch with the Sky and she has four Best of the Net nominations.

Karla Linn Merrifield, a nine-time Pushcart-Prize nominee and National Park Artist-in-Residence, has had 700+ poems appear in dozens of journals and anthologies. She has 14 books to her credit. Following her 2018 *Psyche's Scroll* (Poetry Box Select) is the newly released full-length book *Athabaskan Fractal: Poems of the Far North* from Cirque Press. Her *Godwit: Poems of Canada* (FootHills Publishing) received the Eiseman Award for Poetry. She is a frequent contributor to *The Songs of Eretz Poetry Review*, and assistant editor and poetry book reviewer emerita for *The Centrifugal Eye*.

Bruce Meyer is author of several books of poetry and short fiction. He lives in Barrie, Ontario. In September, Guernica Editions will publish his next collection of poems, McLuhan's Canary, and in 2020 the same press will publish a collection of flash fiction, Down in the Ground.

Christopher Mitchell I am a sort of retired Government Employee who lives in the South. I am married with two adult children. My hobbies are hiking, writing, and proving Mark Twain right about fools and silence.

Shane Moritz teaches writing at the University of Maryland Baltimore County. His poetry has been recognized by the Academy of American Poets among other places.

Michael Neal Morris is the author of *In Domestic* News, *Haiku, Etc, Music for Arguments*, and *Is It I, Rabbi?* Several of his short stories and poems have appeared in print and online publications. He lives with his family outside the Dallas area, and teaches at Eastfield College.

Leah Mueller is an indie writer and spoken word performer from Tacoma, Washington. She is the author of two chapbooks and four books. Her books, "Death and Heartbreak" and "Misguided Behavior" were published in Autumn, 2019 by Weasel Press and Czykmate Press. Leah's work appears in Blunderbuss, The Spectacle, Outlook Springs, Atticus Review, Your Impossible Voice, and other publications. She was a featured poet at the 2015 New York Poetry Festival, and a runner-up in the 2012 Wergle Flomp humor poetry contest.

Naida Mujkić was born in 1984. She holds PhD in Literature and she works as a docent behind the front desks at two university in BiH. She is a member of PEN Center BiH. She was a guest artist at Q21 Museumsquartier Wien and Goten Publishing Skopje. So far, she published 5 books of poetry and one book of lyrical prose. She has participated in several international poetry and literature festivals, such as *Istanbul international poetry and literature festival, 5. Gol Saatleri Şiir Akşamı, 16. Evenings International Sapanca* (Turkey*), 34. Festival des migrations, des cultures et de la Citoyenneté (Luxembourg), SUR (Croatia),* and many more. Also, she had been chosen to present her poetry at the Mediterranea 18 Young Artists Biennale (Albania).

Debjani Mukherjee, an MBA in applied management has a passion for studying human life and puts her observation and feelings into words. Her poems, articles and short stories are published in many international anthologies and magazines. She is a regular contributor to magazines like Setu Mag, GloMag, Destiny Poets, Different Truths, Tuck Magazine, and Stag Hill Literary Journal. Her short story " The Summer Moon won the summer contest of the USA based magazine Academy of heart and mind. Her other short story "The Paper Boat" recently managed to secure its place in the top ten list of the prestigious Bharat Award for literature international.

Hiya Mukherjee was born and brought up in Kolkata, India. She primarily writes in her mother tongue Bengali. Her work has appeared in 'The Disappointed Houswife', 'Plato's Caves Online', 'Cafe Lit' and 'Friday Flash Fiction'. She co-edits 'Agony Opera'-a bilingual bimonthly blogzine. She is currently pursuing her research in theoretical physics.

Sharon Lask Munson was born and raised in Detroit, Michigan. She taught school in England, Germany, Okinawa, and Puerto Rico before driving to Anchorage, Alaska and staying for the next twenty years. She is a retired teacher, poet, coffee addict, old movie enthusiast, lover of road trips—with many published poems, two chapbooks, and two full-length books of poetry. She now lives and writes in Eugene, Oregon. You can find her at www.sharonlaskmunson.com

Cath Nichols' second collection *This is Not a Stunt* was published in 2017 by Valley Press. Stride magazine said it was 'ground-breaking' because of its focus 'on the body... on being different, being transsexual or intersex, and being disabled... Nichols approaches her theme with great skill and a range of poetic forms.' She teaches creative writing p/t at the University of Leeds, UK, and was short-listed for the Hippocrates Award in 2018.

Kirsty A. Niven lives in Dundee, Scotland. Her writing has appeared in anthologies such as *Landfall, A Prince Tribute* and *Of Burgers and Barrooms*. She has also featured in several journals and magazines, including *The Dawntreader, Cicada Magazine, Dundee Writes* and *Word Fountain*. Kirsty's work can also be found online on sites such as Cultured Vultures, Atrium Poetry and Nine Muses Poetry.

Temitope Ogunsina a.k.a topid da poet. Is a performing Poet and journalist from Oyo State, in Oyo town Nigeria. His poetry has been featured in a number of anthologies: I am poetry anthology (2013), fearless poet against bully (2014), Emanation: foray into forever (2014), Spoken ink: written Collection: volume 1(2014),Stolen Flowers (2015),Reclaiming our voices(2015),Poetry Society India anthology (2015),Muse For World peace first edition (2015), Outrage: A protest anthology for injustice in a Post 9/11World(2015), Hark back to ancient and rebuild the world(2015) and in Maganda magazine: Critical Mass(2015) ,The Criterion ; International journal in English Vol.7 issues 1(2016).Muse for World peace 2nd edition (2016), Cluster Magazine 1st edition (2016),Emanation: I am not a number (2017), Cluster Magazine 2nd edition (2017)

Keli Osborn lives in western Oregon, where she volunteers with community organizations, writes essays and poetry, and grows raspberries, grapes and other deliciousness. Her writing has appeared in the Timberline Review, Confrontation, Passager and other journals, and in several anthologies including All We Can Hold: Poems of Motherhood and Nasty Women Poets: An Unapologetic Anthology of Subversive Verse.

Carl "Papa" Palmer of Old Mill Road in Ridgeway, Virginia, lives in University Place, Washington. He is retired from the military and Federal Aviation Administration (FAA) enjoying life now as "Papa" to his grand descendants and being a Franciscan Hospice volunteer. Carl is a Pushcart Prize and Micro Award nominee. MOTTO: Long Weekends Forever!

Larry Pike's poetry and fiction has appeared in *Aethlon: The Journal of Sport Literature, The Louisville Review, Hospital Drive, Seminary Ridge Review, Caesura, Amethyst Review, Exposition Review, Vitamin ZZZ* and other publications. He lives in Glasgow, Kentucky.

Jaclyn Piudik is the author of *TO SUTURE WHAT FRAYS* (Kelsay Books 2017) and two chapbooks, *OF GAZELLES UNHEARD* (Beautiful Outlaw 2013) and *THE TAO OF LOATHLINESS* (fooliar press 2005/8). Her poems have appeared in numerous anthologies and journals, including *New American Writing, Columbia Poetry Review, Burning House* and *Contemporary Verse 2*. She received a New York Times Fellowship for Creative Writing and the Sellers Award from the Academy of American Poets. Piudik holds an M.A. in Creative Writing from the City College of New York, as well as a Ph.D. in Medieval Studies from the University of Toronto.

Stephanie Pressman earned an MA in English from San Jose State University, taught writing at community college, and became a graphic artist and owner of her own design and publishing business, Frog on the Moon. An active member of Poetry Center San Jose since its founding, she served as co-editor and layout artist of *cæsura*. She also co-edited *americas review*. Her work has appeared in many journals including *Bridges, cæsura, CQ/California State Poetry Quarterly*, and *Montserrat Review*. Her long poem *Lovebirdman* appears in an illustrated volume published in June, 2018 (available on Amazon).

Deborah Purdy lives outside Philadelphia where she writes poetry and creates fiber art. Her poems have appeared in Gravel, Cleaver Magazine, The American Poetry Journal, and other publications.

Elaine Reardon is a poet, herbalist, educator, and member of the Society of Children's Book Writers & Illustrators. Her chapbook, The Heart is a Nursery For Hope, won first honors from Flutter Press in 2016. In 2018 Elaine won the Beal Poetry Prize (11/18), was a Writer's Digest finalist, and was shortlisted at the Hammond House Poetry contest in England. Most recently Elaine's poetry and essays have been published by Crossways Journal, UCLA journal, Automatic Pilot, Sleep-ZZZ Journal,Rufous.Salon.com, and several anthologies in Europe. She has a website at elainereardon.wordpress.com.

Shelly Rodrigue's poems have appeared in GTK Creative Journal, the Borfski Press, Fourth & Sycamore, Ellipsis, New Reader Magazine, and Ms. Aligned 2: Women Writing About Men, an anthology. She is the 2017 recipient of the Andrea Saunders Gereighty/Academy of American Poets Poetry Award. Currently, she teaches ESL online for VIPKID.

Jennifer Rood teaches and writes in Southern Oregon and has fond memories of her grandmother's kitchen and small farm in East Tennessee, where she was always welcomed in with hugs and a table full of food made with love. She has published in various journals and anthologies and serves on the Board of the Oregon Poetry Association.

Iris N. Schwartz's fiction has been published in dozens of journals and anthologies including *Anti-Heroin Chic, Blink-Ink, Fictive Dream,* and *Jellyfish Review.* Her short-short story collection, *My Secret Life with Chris Noth,* published in 2017, was nominated for two Pushcart Prizes. *Shame,* which contains the Best Micro Fiction 2018-nominated story "Dogs," is her latest collection.

Raven Sky is a polyamorous queer femme who hails from Canada and who is fueled by wanderlust, tea, books, and insatiable curiosity. She's published erotic poetry in Pan's Ex: Queer Sex Poetry, as well as erotic short stories in the following anthologies: Best Lesbian Erotica Vol. 3, Escape to Pleasure: Lesbian Travel Erotica, and Lust in the Dust: Post-Apocalyptic Erotica.

Zigzagging back and forth across the Canadian/US border, Adrian Slonaker works as a copywriter and copy editor. Adrian's work has been nominated for Best of the Net and has appeared in *Pangolin Review, Aerodrome, WINK: Writers in the Know* and others.

Samuel Swauger is a poet from Baltimore, Maryland. Some of his work appears in the magazines Wordgathering, Third Wednesday, and the Front Porch Review. His website is samuelswauger.com and his Twitter is @samuelswauger.

Nicole Taylor lives in Eugene, Oregon. She is an artist, a hiker, a poetry note taker, a sketcher, a volunteer and a dancer, formerly in Salem's DanceAbility. Her poems has been accepted in Boneshaker: A Bicycling Almanac, Camel Saloon; Cirque Journal; Clackamas Literary Review; Just Another Art Movement Journal - New Zealand, West Wind Review and others. You can read more her poetry at oregonpoeticvoices.org/poet/312/.a collection of Oregon poets with written and audio poetry available online through Lewis & Clark College in Portland.

Born and raised in Utah, Ginger Lee Thomason currently lives in

Cambridge, England. She is working on her PhD in Creative Writing at Anglia Ruskin University, under the supervision of Dr. Tiffani Angus. She also has a professional background in higher and public education administration and with the US Federal Government. For her PhD, she has written a novel titled *How to Cook a* Dragon, which can be described as "Masterchef in Middle-Earth." The accompanying academic portion will be about food in fantasy sub creation. Previous publications include "Layton, Utah" in *Reaching Beyond the Saguaros*, by Serving House Books, and poems published in the *Icarus Down Review* and the *Yellow Chair Review*. For more works please visit www.gingerleethomason.com.

Mikal Trimm has sold over 50 short stories and 100 poems to numerous venues including Postscripts, Strange Horizons, Realms of Fantasy, and Ellery Queen's Mystery Magazine.

Todd C. Truffin is a poet and teacher. His work has been seen in *Pilgrimage*, *The Lamp-Post*, and the IPPY award-winning anthology *O! Relentless Death!: Celebrities, Loss, and a Year of Mourning*.

Yrik-Max Valentonis is a writer and cartoonist. His comics and writings have appeared in magazines, e-zines, radio broadcasts, art exhibitions: Brave New Word, Chaleur Magazine, Cliterature, Experimental-Experimental-Literature, FreezeRay, Maintenant, Utsanga, and Zoomoozophone, the chapbooks: *iDEAL* and *this is visual poetry*; the anthologies: *Animal Blessings*, *Beer-Battered Shrimp for Cognitive Ruminations*, *Divided Again*, *Sinbad and the Winds of Destiny*, and *Zombie Nation: St. Pete*. He earned a BA in English and American Literature from the University of South Florida and a MFA in Poetry & Prose from Naropa University. Yrik-Max Valentonis wanders through the urban landscape seeking out fairy circles. He makes puppets so other people can see his imaginary friends. He steals apples to justify his philosophy. He is Baba Yaga's favorite grandson.

Edward Vidaurre, the 2018-2019 McAllen,Texas Poet Laureate and author of six collections of poetry: JAZzHOUSE (Prickly Pear Publishing 2019) is his latest with WHEN A CITY ENDS, forthcoming from King Shot Press. He writes from the front lines of the Mexican-American borderlands of the Rio Grande Valley in south Texas and Publisher/Editor of FlowerSong Books.

Vivian Wagner lives in New Concord, Ohio, where she's an associate professor of English at Muskingum University. Her work has appeared in *Slice Magazine, Muse/A Journal, Forage Poetry Journal, Pittsburgh Poetry Review, McSweeney's Internet Tendency, Gone Lawn, The Atlantic, Narratively, The Ilanot Review, Silk Road Review, Zone 3,Bending Genres*, and other publications. She's the author of a memoir, *Fiddle: One Woman, Four Strings, and 8,000 Miles of Music* (Citadel-Kensington); a full-length poetry collection, *Raising* (Clare Songbirds Publishing House); and three poetry chapbooks: *The Village* (Aldrich Press-Kelsay Books), *Making* (Origami Poems Project), and *Curiosities* (Unsolicited Press).

Barrett Warner is the author of *Why Is It So Hard to Kill You?* (Somondoco, 2016) and *My Friend Ken Harvey* (Publishing Genius, 2014). He lives on the South Edisto River in SC.

Suellen Wedmore, Poet Laureate *emerita* for the seaside town of Rockport, Massachusetts, has been widely published. She has been awarded first place in the *Writer's Digest's* Rhyming Poem Contest and, most recently, in the Digest's Non-Rhyming Poems contest. Her chapbook *Deployed* won the Grayson Press annual contest, her chapbook *On Marriage and Other Parallel Universes* was published by Finishing Line Press, and her chapbook *Mind the Light* won first place in Quill's Edge Press's "Women on the Edge" contest. In 2014 she won first place in the Studios of Key West Contest, and three of her poems have been nominated for a Pushcart Prize. After working for many years as a speech and language therapist in the Rockport Schools. she retired to pursue a Master of Fine Arts in Poetry, graduating from New England College in 2004.

Julia Wendell's memoir, "Come to the X," will be published by Galileo Press this year. She is the author of seven collections of poems, most recently "Take This Spoon," from Main Street Rag Press, in which the poems in this anthology first appeared.

Joe Williams is a writer and performing poet from Leeds, UK. In 2017 his debut pamphlet, 'Killing the Piano', was published by Half Moon Books, and he won the Open Mic Competition at Ilkley Literature Festival. His second book, the verse novella 'An Otley Run', was published in November 2018, and was shortlisted in the Best Novella category at the 2019 Saboteur Awards.

André Le Mont Wilson was born in Los Angeles the son of poets. After their deaths in 2012, he began writing poetry. He has published in *sPARKLE + bLINK* and *Not Your Mother's Breast Milk*, and was anthologized in *Civil Liberties United*. He received a Pushcart Prize nomination in 2018.

Eduard Schmidt-Zorner is an artist and a translator and writer of poetry, crime novels and short stories. He is writing haibun, tanka, haiku and poetry in four languages: English, French, Spanish and German and holds workshops on Japanese and Chinese style poetry and prose. He is a member of four writer groups in Ireland and lives in County Kerry, Ireland, since more than 25 years and is a proud Irish citizen, born in Germany. He was published in 46 anthologies, literary journals and broadsheets in UK, Ireland, Canada and USA. Writes also under his pen name: Eadbhard McGowan.

Editor Bios

Karen Cline-Tardiff has been writing since she could hold a pen. She writes poetry, flash fiction, personal essays, short stories, and grant requests. She has been published in a variety of online and print outlets. She was born in Texas, lived a little bit of everywhere, and now resides on the Texas Gulf Coast. When she can't find poetry somewhere, she puts it there.

Jennifer Taylor is a daughter of Texas, residing, now, near Iowa State University. She volunteers with creative writing and English students, and especially enjoys working with those for whom English is not their first language. She loves all things artsy, and describes herself, artistically speaking, as the proverbial jack of all trades, master of none, having been, at various times, a writer, poet, painter, dancer, singer, choir director, theater producer, choreographer and, obviously, editor.

Made in the USA
Columbia, SC
09 January 2020